Clones – Book One

By Laurann Dohner

F Clones

by Laurann Dohner

Figures

When one of his friends goes missing, Figures needs to masquerade as a human visiting a space station. It would cost him his life if he's caught. Humans hate and fear clones that much. He doesn't discover what happened to Blade, but he does find a sweet, elderly human who makes him smile.

Anna left Earth to cross off the last thing on her bucket list. She saw the stars, traveled on a pleasure cruiser, and completed her trip by ending up on a space station. She believes her adventures are over until she meets a handsome clone.

And he gives her a second chance at life in a new clone body.

Free

Marisol did the unthinkable by falling in love with a clone. Her grandfather is the owner of Clone World. He'd rather see them both dead than allow them to be together. The plan was simple. She would help Free and five other clones escape and would join them later. Only, it didn't work out that way.

Free, once known as Freak, lost the love of his life when she didn't join him. When he receives word that Marisol is looking for him, he'll do anything to get her back. Anything.

Clones Series List

B Clones

F Clones

F Clones by Laurann Dohner

Copyright © June 2024

Editor: Kelli Collins

Cover Art: Dar Albert

ISBN: 978-1-950597-31-4

ALL RIGHTS RESERVED. The unauthorized reproduction or distribution of this copyrighted work is illegal, except for the case of brief quotations in reviews and articles.

Criminal copyright infringement is investigated by the FBI and is punishable by up to 5 years in federal prison and a fine of $250,000.

All characters and events in this book are fictitious. Any resemblance to actual persons living or dead is coincidental.

Chapter One	8
Chapter Two	26
Chapter Three	37
Chapter Four	47
Chapter Five	58
Chapter Six	71
Chapter Seven	85
Chapter Eight	98
Chapter Nine	112
Chapter Ten	122
Prologue	130
Chapter One	138
Chapter Two	151
Chapter Three	161
Chapter Four	171
Chapter Five	189
Chapter Six	201
Chapter Seven	211
Chapter Eight	226
Chapter Nine	239
Chapter Ten	251

F Clones

Clones – Book Two

By Laurann Dohner

Figures

Chapter One

Three Months Ago

Figures, otherwise known as Fig, eased onto the barstool and kept his head down. There was no sign of the law enforcement authorities on Riddle Station. The distinctive uniforms they wore were easy to spot with their dark green, armor-shelled bodies. It made him breathe easier. He'd be killed if they realized he was a clone.

He'd grown his blond hair long, and dressing as a maintenance worker helped him blend in with the humans. It was a perfect disguise. Stations usually hired dozens of them every month since most didn't stick with the job for long.

His shoulders were hunched, and the padding over his stomach helped him appear slightly out of shape. No one spared him a second glance when he visited various establishments since he'd arrived earlier in the day.

Fig had overheard a lot of conversations. Earth had raised prices on everything. Some stores were now buying food and merchandise from colony planets to save money. The civilians and visitors complained because, either way, they felt they were being ripped off.

There had been a fire a week prior on deck nine that had killed six people. Emerson, whoever he was, had finally been caught by his wife for visiting the brothel on deck two. She had filed for divorce. Fig got the strong impression that Emerson wasn't well-liked since the humans talking about him had snickered and laughed.

No one had mentioned a clone. It would have been huge news if one had been captured or killed. Part of Fig was relieved, but he also was worried. *Where is my friend? What has happened to Blade?* He'd checked out every ship docked at Riddle first thing. None of them were the *Barnel*. His friend's shuttle wasn't there.

One bit of helpful information he'd overheard was about how stripped, dead ships found abandoned in space were dumped on a moon named Hubble. That would be his next stop. He really hoped he didn't find the *Barnel* there. It would mean that Blade must be dead. Grief tugged at his heart. He wasn't willing to give up hope for his friend yet. That meant sticking around to spy more.

Big, one of his fellow clones, had asked if he'd help search for their missing friend. Six of them had escaped Clone World together. They'd made an abandoned mining operation station their home base.

Six males living together had been difficult after a while. They all had strong personalities, and twinned with boredom, they'd begun to argue a lot. Five of them had left to seek adventures.

All five kept in contact with Big. He'd been the one to remain living full-time at the mining station. It was highly alarming to learn that none of them had heard from Blade in so long. It was also out of character. All they had was each other. They might have had a difficult time living together, but they always checked in.

Fig walked into a drinking establishment. Drunk humans tended to gossip the most. If he didn't hear about a clone from them, he would leave the station. The lighting inside the bar wasn't the greatest as he crossed the room and took a seat at the counter. That was just the way he liked it. It would be tough for anyone to get a good look at him.

The bartender paused before him. "What is your pleasure?"

Fig didn't know the names of drinks sold in bars. "Something cold, smooth, and strong. Surprise me."

"Sure thing, mister."

Fig relaxed a minute later when a tall glass slid his way. It was some blue concoction with fog slowly rolling out the top. He slapped down the money and wrapped his hand around the glass. It was icy to the touch. "Thanks. Keep the change."

He lifted the glass and took a sip. It tasted a bit minty but was good. He swallowed and listened to the chaos surrounding him. At least fifty people had to be sardined inside the confined space, and all seemed to be conversing.

He'd missed watching people having a good time and interacting with others. That had been an everyday occurrence on Clone World. They always had a heavy influx of tourists the clones served. Most of his time now was spent living in silence on his shuttle. Occasionally, he'd tune into public broadcasts coming from planets or space stations just to hear other voices when he flew near one.

He tried to focus on the important things when loneliness hit. No one on Clone World controlled his every action any longer. He wasn't being abused by the whims of paying guests or the human staff. His current life might have been boring, but he was free.

Big's news about finding a female clone had split his feelings over the matter in two directions. Half of him was ecstatically delighted that the male had found someone to love. Big was a good male who deserved happiness. The other half was envious.

The chances of one of them coming across a clone being shipped without a convoy of protection was near impossible. It would be suicide to take on multiple ships to raid those types of shipments.

Gemma had been an illegally created clone being flown to Clone World under the radar. Big had been extremely lucky that he'd gone to steal plasma and discovered her in that cargo hold, too.

A longing hit to sit at one of the gaming tables to hold an actual conversation. He resisted. There was taking a risk and being outright stupid. Desperation to find his fellow missing clone friend had brought him to the station, but it would be pure idiocy to expose himself to humans by interacting directly with them. He'd just have to enjoy being close to the action but not being a part of it.

Fig took a sip of his drink, contemplating what he'd do after hopefully discovering what had happened to Blade. The loneliness was really starting to get to him. It might be time to return to the mining station.

He had no doubt that Big would welcome him home with open arms. Then again, he didn't want to become a third wheel. Seeing the couple together might add to his misery when he'd never have that.

Motion to his left had him reaching for his hidden weapon inside his pocket in case it was needed. A smaller body slid onto the barstool next to him a few minutes later. He darted a look to make certain they weren't a threat.

Few things surprised him, but the woman who placed her large bag on the counter next to him did. She was extremely advanced in years and wore colorful clothing. Her shirt was bright yellow, and the long skirt was an energetic blue. It was obvious that the human wasn't an authority or a danger. He lowered his guard a bit.

"Hi. I'm Anna." She held out a frail, wrinkled hand in his direction.

Figures wasn't sure what to do, but she might draw attention if he pretended not to hear her. He released his weapon and twisted a little in his seat to gently clasp her hand.

He took a closer look at her and met a pair of very lively green eyes. Deep wrinkles creased her face, and stark white hair framed her features. He could still tell she'd once been attractive.

"Hi."

She clung to him instead of just giving his hand an obligatory pump. "You're so warm, and my, you have big hands." She leaned in a little closer, squinting at him. "My vision isn't so good anymore. I swear, in the last two years, I've gone as blind as a bat. Wow. You're a handsome fella. I bet your mother has to beat the girls away from you."

"Thank you." He was grateful that she assumed he had parents.

Anna released his hand. "I hope you don't mind me sitting here. You were alone, and it's hard to find someone who will talk to an old lady like me. Are you up for some company? I'm harmless." She flashed a sweet smile.

He grinned over the invitation. "I'd like that."

"You'd be in serious trouble, though, if I were fifty years younger." She lifted her hand to wave at the bartender. He approached, and she ordered a drink. Anna dug into her purse to pay for it. "I've learned since I arrived here that they rob you at this station. Everything is so darn expensive."

"You don't live here?"

"Not really. I just arrived a few days ago. This is my last destination, though."

That news disappointed him a little. He wouldn't be able to ask her if she'd heard anything about a clone being discovered or arrested over the past year. She was too new to the station.

She accepted the drink and took a sip. "They have good beer." She turned to face him and encroached into his personal space to squint at him again.

He leaned closer, hoping it would help her see better. That earned him another smile from her. "You are settling here?"

"Settling? No. I'm just about out of money. I sold my house and cashed in my retirement stock to see space. I only have a few weeks left to live. I found a nice little rental room that is paid for until next month. I'll be toes up by then."

She surprised Fig again. "You're dying?"

"It's my heart. I'm not going into details because it's boring, and you shouldn't have to hear what age does to a body when you're young. I had no chance of buying a new heart to have mine replaced since you have to be mega-rich to afford that. I opted to take pills to keep my ticker going. I stopped taking them days ago when I ran out. The doc assured me I wouldn't make it more than two weeks afterward."

"I'm sorry."

She reached out and patted his chest. "Don't be. This has been the most adventurous thing I've ever done in my life." She smiled. "Leaving Earth was the one and only item on my bucket list."

"A what?"

"Bucket list. It means making a list of what you want to do before you die. I knew it was coming, so I got off my ass and sold everything. It was enough to follow my one and only dream. I did it. It was worth it, too. I've seen three planets and spent two months on a huge pleasure cruiser, and this is my fourth station. I like this one. The last one was boring. They didn't have a bar. What's the point of dying if you can't do the things that are bad for you, like drinking?"

He grinned, charmed by the older female. "That's true."

"I know it. You should have heard my friends." She shook her head. "They said I must have lost my mind to want to see outer space. I sure wasn't going to allow the government to steal everything I worked so hard for if I'd stayed there to die. That's what they do to people without any family left. I was going to spend every dime and see all the things I've always dreamed about. I've done that."

Fig's humor had faded while listening to her. "No one is traveling with you?"

"Don't you worry. What's the worst that could happen?" She chuckled. "I'm already dying. Nothing beats that."

"You could be targeted by thieves."

She shrugged. "I don't have much to steal. My rent is paid, and three meals a day come with it." She leaned in closer. "Besides, if they are willing to put their hands on my bod, I might get a thrill." She winked.

He knew his mouth parted as he gaped at her.

She laughed. "Don't be so serious. You're too handsome for that. That was a joke. Nobody wants to touch me. Trust me. It's been twenty years since my Ralph died, and no man beat down my door to climb into my bed after he was gone. My husband of forty-two years didn't even want to touch me near the end. I married a man much older than me. His lower half stopped working long before his heart went."

Fig had no words, stunned. He was sure she'd just said her husband wasn't physically able to have sex with her. *Is that a thing with humans? I learn something new every day.*

Music came on, and Anna swayed a little in her seat. "That's nice. I like to dance. Do as much of it as you can while you're young. I didn't catch your name. Mind sharing it, or should I just call you handsome?"

She did amuse him. "You can call me Fig."

"I like that. It's kind of sexy. It makes me think of a fig leaf. That doesn't hide much on a man."

He laughed, understanding what a leaf was, if not the exact tree it would come from. "No, I guess it wouldn't."

"As I said, it's lucky for you that I'm not fifty years younger. I was once a looker. Forget my twenties. I still had bad acne, and all those hormones were hell. I think I was kind of a bitch until I mellowed at thirty. That was my favorite year. Most women dread hitting the big three zero, but not me. Mature enough to be wise but young enough to want to enjoy life still."

"Did you have a good life?"

"I wish." She took another sip of her drink. "Ralph kept me reigned in. His idea of excitement was watching a game for entertainment and barking out orders that usually involved me making him food. Here's a tip for you: Life is too short to be miserable. Change it before you find yourself old and with regrets. I've got plenty of those."

"Like what?" He was enjoying their talk. She fascinated him with the things she said and the information about herself that she just blurted out. It was as if she decided to keep no secrets private.

"You don't really want to hear me go off about that. It's nice of you to ask. I bet you have better things to do than spending more time with me. Thank you for not rushing off right away. I appreciate that. I was getting a little lonesome."

"I know all about that. I work by myself. There's no one to spend time with. I like talking with you."

She reached out and rubbed his arm. "You shouldn't be alone. Find yourself a woman. It won't be hard with your good looks."

A bit of bitterness surfaced. "That's not true. My station in life isn't something that draws someone to me."

She shook her head. "Young people these days are stupid. I would have chased you down and caught you if I'd met you when I was your age. Then again, I never knew someone who looked like you do, or I might have divorced Ralph to talk you into marrying me. You're a sweetheart for putting up with an old lady. I couldn't even get my husband to say more than two sentences in a row that didn't involve food or to complain about something."

"Why did you stay married to him?"

"I made a commitment, and I always keep my word, come hell or high water. I suffered both, but I stayed until the end. I tried to make it as pleasant as possible, but Ralph wasn't a happy person. We were fire and water. He put me out." She laughed. "In so many ways. You need a pretty girl in your life, Fig. Make her laugh, treat her good, and she'll be yours forever."

He wished it were that simple. The idea of having someone to share his life with made his chest ache with longing. It was terrible to always be alone. It left him too much time to think of everything he wanted but would never obtain.

A slower song came on the speakers around the bar, and Anna swayed again in her chair. She seemed to really enjoy the song.

He slid off the barstool. "Would you like to dance with me?"

Her eyes widened. "Oh, why couldn't I have met you when I was young?" She glanced around. "I don't want to embarrass you."

"I don't care about what anyone thinks. You're the only person I know here."

He ended up helping her off her chair. She was so frail that he worried she might slip and fall. The smile on her face when he pulled her out onto the nearly empty dance floor warmed his heart. The top of her head didn't reach his shoulders, but she put one hand there, and he offered her his other to hold.

"I'm not good at this. It's my first time. Be gentle with me," he teased. "I'll avoid stepping on your feet, though. I've seen people dance before."

She leaned in as they started to slow-step in a circle. Anna rested her cheek against his chest. "Thank you so much for doing this. You don't know what this means to me."

He did. The basic lack of physical contact and the burden of constantly being alone tended to get to a person after a while. It caused depression and a lack of motivation to sometimes get out of bed. He wrapped his arm around her frail waist a little tighter in case she needed the extra support.

"Where's a time machine when I need one?"

"What does that mean?"

She lifted her chin and smiled. "I'm telling you, Fig. You'd be in serious trouble if I were thirty again. I'd climb you like a tree and keep hold of you."

"A tree?" He was amused again.

"That's probably too outdated a saying for someone your age. It means I'd be all over you. I might be old, but I'm not dead yet. Those regrets I mentioned wouldn't be so many if I'd had a nice man like you in my life."

"Tell me about what you would change if you could."

"I don't want to make you blush. That's no way to thank you for doing a good deed for the elderly." She suddenly stopped dancing.

"What's wrong?"

"Nothing."

She released his shoulder and reached up, her fingers curling behind his neck. She gently tugged. He lowered his head until their faces were closer. He guessed she wanted to get a better look at him.

"Oh, sweetheart. Who put that sadness in your pretty blue eyes? I couldn't see so well at that dark bar, but the lights are brighter here. Did some woman break your heart?"

"I'm fine."

She kept peering at him. "You're not. I know that look. I see it all the time in the mirror. It's called misery."

"I'm tired of always being alone," he admitted. The admission had just burst out of him. She was a human being who was kind to him. It was a first.

She released his neck but kept hold of his hand. Anna turned, and he followed her back to their seats. He helped her onto her barstool before retaking his own. She leaned in closer and placed her palm on his arm.

"You need to change that. Trust me on this, Fig. I lived with a man for forty-two years who made me feel wretched. Do you know why? He didn't know how to love. I'd become so afraid of rejection by the time he died that I didn't take a chance to end up with another man who could give me what I craved. Everyone should know love and be the center of someone's world."

Her words made him feel bad for her.

"You deserve that," she continued. "Don't take this wrong, but you've got the kind of body a woman has fantasies about. Believe me. I am earning a seat in hell right now for noticing that, but it's the truth. You're handsome, and you're a really good man. I know that because you're being so generous to me."

"Thank you for saying that. You're too kind."

"No. I'm just a crazy old lady you met in a bar, but you've been kinder to me than any man ever has. Go find someone who thinks the way I do. She'll stick with you through thick and thin if you open your heart to her."

"No woman is going to want to be with me."

"Bullshit. I'm not blowing smoke up your ass. I am too old to waste my time being polite for no good reason."

He laughed. "Is that another saying? Smoke up your ass?"

"Yes." She smiled. "It means I'm not saying it just to be nice. I mean it. You're a new regret, Fig. I wish I were young right now because I'd demand you take me wherever you call home, and I'd show you that you're wrong."

The female made him feel good with her kind words. She wasn't done speaking yet, though, as she continued.

"You couldn't shake me off with a stick. It means I'd just move in and show you all the wonderful things in life that you're obviously missing." She rubbed his arm. "You need to look for someone to share your life with. Just be yourself, and she'll fall in love."

He leaned in. "Can I tell you a secret?"

"You can tell me anything. I don't have anyone else to share whatever you say with."

He hesitated and lowered his voice. "I'm a clone."

She blinked, but he could see that she'd heard him. Her body had tensed.

He backed away. "That's why I'm destined to be alone. I can't give a woman children, and she'll never see me as a man. She'd think I'm a thing instead of a person with emotions. I should go. If anyone realizes what I am, they'll arrest and sentence me to death. Thank you for talking to me."

She clutched at his shirt and almost fell out of her seat to keep a hold of him. He worried that she'd scream out a warning of what he was to the other humans in the room. He couldn't let her fall, though. He gripped Anna's hips and placed her more firmly on the stool.

"Don't go. You're a person, Fig. You're a good man. That's all that matters."

He stared into her eyes, seeing no deception there.

"You're not a thing. Don't let anyone ever say that to you. Don't even think that way. It's bullshit. Promise me that you'll look for a woman to share your life with. She's out there. You just need to find her. Let her get to know you, and she won't care about something that silly."

"Silly?" He was astounded that she'd use that description.

She nodded. "I know a lot of assholes who were birthed the old-fashioned way. You're a thousand times more human than they are. My husband hated kids, and I still signed up for that. He wasn't a tenth of the man you are. You just danced with an old lady to get me to smile. That makes you pretty special."

"Thank you for saying that, Anna."

"I mean it."

"You cheater!" a man yelled, and a table crashed to the floor on the other side of the dance floor.

It happened so fast. Fig spun to see what was going on, but a loud blast filled the room. One of the men who'd been playing cards now stood and held a weapon. A second man sitting in a chair hit the floor, a hole torn through his chest from the laser blast. Other men jumped on the one holding the weapon. They tore it out of his hand and took him to the ground.

Fig needed to leave. The authorities would be called, wanting everyone to make statements. They might ask for identification. He turned back to Anna.

Her mouth was open, her eyes wide. She lowered her head, and he followed her gaze. The laser had gone through the man seated at the destroyed table and into her side, where her arm was still lifted to hold her drink. Her hand gripping his shirt eased until she let go.

He grabbed Anna before she fell over and cradled her in his arms. "Get help. She's been hit," Fig yelled at the bartender.

"Fig?"

He looked down at Anna's face. All the color seemed to leach out of her wrinkled cheeks. "Hang on, Anna. I'll carry you to their medical facility."

She reached up and touched his face. "Don't. This is the best way to go. You're holding me, and I'm not alone. Thank you. When I'm gone, go find that woman. Promise me."

He opened his mouth, ready to say anything she wanted to hear. Anna's eyes closed before he could, and her hand dropped. He used his elbow and shoved her purse aside, laying her flat on the top of the bar counter. She wasn't breathing anymore. He checked the wound and saw the extent of the damage. There was no way to save her.

"Fuck." The bartender came over. "Is she dead?"

It took seconds for Fig to answer, so horrified and stunned by what had just happened. "Yes."

"Is she a relation to you?"

"No."

"Just leave her. She's not a resident, and I know she's staying in the B section on deck two. Maintenance will come to get rid of her body."

"What?" Fig was in shock over how Anna had died like that. It had happened too fast for his mind to process.

"B section means she's poor. Someone like her doesn't have family who would pay for a decent funeral. We get a lot of fights in here, so the clean-up crew will just toss her body into the furnace with the trash."

That outraged Fig. "No. I'll see that she gets a proper funeral." It would mean he'd have to stick around until the authorities cleared the scene, but he wasn't allowing that kind of cruelty to happen to Anna's body. She wouldn't be disposed of like trash.

"Then take her body and go to section C on deck five. There's a morgue there, and they can arrange something for the right price."

Fig glanced around. The man who'd fired the weapon was gone. "Aren't the authorities going to investigate?"

The bartender snorted. "Where in the hell do you think you are? We don't have a judge, and nobody wants to pay to transport that piece of shit to somewhere that does. Justice will be served when he's tossed into the trash furnace for killing two people. I'm sure that's where they dragged him off. Weapons aren't allowed to be fired on the station, and murder is an instant death sentence. Case closed."

He looked down at Anna.

"Hang on. I've got a tarp around here somewhere. You don't want people staring at you for carrying a body through the station. It wouldn't be the first time, but some tourists get upset. A large pleasure cruiser docked half an hour ago. I don't want them to see you coming out of my bar with her and think it's a dangerous place to visit. It's bad for business." The bartender walked away but returned a minute later. "Here. Wrap her and go."

Pure rage gripped Fig. He hated to put Anna in a tarp, but he had no choice. He didn't want to draw more attention to himself. He gently eased her wrapped body over his shoulder and picked up her purse. He wasn't leaving it behind for thieves to take. Anna hadn't deserved to die that way. She should be alive and smiling. It wasn't fair.

He exited the bar and lowered his chin to hide his features as much as possible when large groups of people milled between the shops. He reached the wide corridor that led to his shuttle and turned. Nine other ships shared the docking sleeve.

"Hey!" A man grinned at him. He'd set up his wares right in front of where his ship had docked. "Fresh meat."

Fig kept walking.

"It's as fresh as the day it was slaughtered. The butcher cuts them up, and they go into instant cryo freeze. It's like he handed it to you right over the counter."

Fig stopped and noticed the cryo freezers for the first time. The vendor had half a dozen small ones laid out, marking what kind of product he had available.

"Do you have anything larger?"

"Yes, sir. Are you from the pleasure cruiser? I've got entire cows stored inside my ship. It would make a hell of a feast for your most important passengers. I take all forms of payment. You could charge it to your company. My cryo units have air hover. You can borrow some and deliver the meat right to your ship's kitchen."

A plan instantly formed. Fig was tired of life fucking him over, but the last straw had been Anna. She'd braved leaving Earth to have her one last adventure, and she'd been nice to him. Her words had given him hope that things could get better. Maybe she'd been right.

"Show me this cow."

Chapter Two

The Present

Fig always experienced an adrenaline rush when he attacked a DJD Clone Corp transport with his shuttle and took out their engines. He hadn't always been a thief. He'd become one after escaping from Clone World. It was the only way to survive. He'd grown quite skilled at space piracy.

DJD Clone Corp made a fortune selling living beings and made those clones dependent on needing specially designed plasma every three months. It was not only how they kept their creations enslaved but ensured a steady stream of profit. A clone's body began to deteriorate and break down without those transfusions. Only legal owners of clones could purchase that plasma to keep their investments alive.

It was a bonus that Fig got to steal from an extremely wealthy human who'd made owning clones his business empire. Clone World had become one of the top vacation spots for other rich people. He held no sympathy for Rico Florigo. That's also why he felt zero guilt about using Clone World funds to order what was on the transport he was currently targeting. That money was owed to him for all he'd previously endured. It wasn't like clones were paid wages.

His mind switched to thoughts of Anna. She'd haunted him since her death. He'd finally met a human who'd seen him as a real person instead of something to fear or loathe. She hadn't deserved to be murdered. It had spurred him into doing something drastic and dangerous.

Fig's next thought was about how grateful he'd been after getting word that Blade was alive. His fellow clone had been forced to live with human criminals until he'd escaped the space pirates to rescue a human. Both were now safely living on the abandoned mining station with Big and his female, Gemma.

Fig docked with the transport he'd disabled the engines on and checked his weapons as he left the cockpit. Live guards wouldn't be traveling on a lone ship, but sometimes there were automated defense systems to deal with.

He'd checked the manifest twice. The container he sought was listed as cargo. The difficult part had been waiting for it to ship from Earth. Patience wasn't something Fig had much of. Every day had dragged on as he'd repeatedly waited for the shipment to leave Earth and be sent toward Clone World.

Fig shorted out the door to the transport's cargo port and forced it open. An alarm blared inside as he drew his weapon. He inched inside, scanning for any signs of movement. There were none.

He glanced up at the ceiling. His mouth pressed into a grim line when he spotted the automated motion lasers. He fired at both, taking them out before they took shots at him.

He made one more sweep to make certain he'd destroyed any threats before he strode forward. He'd memorized the crate label number in case they were shipping plasma in the larger cryo units.

He found four that were the right size and shape. He read off the first label, but it wasn't the one he sought. It turned out to be the third one. He smiled.

"Finally."

He bent down and found the controls. It was tempting to rip it open to get to the contents, but he wanted to reach a safer location first. The transport ship's computer pilot would be sending out a distress signal after being attacked. There weren't any other ships in the vicinity, but this was one time he wasn't willing to risk someone responding and him getting into a fight.

He turned on the mini hover jets, and the large unit lifted from the floor once he cut the straps. He grabbed the handle and pulled, leading it over to his own ship. He returned to the cargo hold of the transport. Fig needed to grab a few of the smaller units holding plasma. He wanted to stockpile as much as possible so he wouldn't have to hit another transport for a long time.

The alarm on his wrist vibrated, and he cursed. The long-range sensors had picked up traffic. He didn't take the time to hover the unit closest to him. Fig just hefted the heavy freezer unit and carried it back to his shuttle, thankful for his clone strength. He dumped it inside his hold but didn't bother to close the other hatch. He sealed his side of the shuttle and ran toward the cockpit.

He detached from the transport as soon as his ass landed in the seat and took off fast. He didn't care about the cargo he'd left behind being destroyed. He'd grabbed what mattered and enough extra clone plasma to make sure he wouldn't need to steal more for at least a year.

Sensors showed another ship in the distance, but it was too small to be an authority cruiser. He quickly deduced that it was probably a privately owned shuttle carrying passengers to visit Clone World. It was a very popular human vacation destination spot.

The other option was it could be a pirate team. If so, they'd quickly realize he wasn't some rich human tourist when they came across the destroyed supply transport. Not many humans bothered to attack them since they wouldn't gain any profit. Clone plasma was deadly to humans, and no one wanted to buy it on the black market. Wealthy owners of clones couldn't be sure it was the real stuff and didn't want their expensive property dying.

He burned thrusters hard in case it was pirates coming after his shuttle, regardless of what they'd consider worthless cargo. There was no way he'd allow anyone to take what he'd stolen. Sensors suddenly showed the other ship again. Then it disappeared.

Figs cursed, knowing what the other ship was doing. The pilot wasn't skilled enough to prevent his sensors from registering their presence. It just confirmed that it must be a pirate team. They were known to group together in larger numbers, forming gangs. Whoever was out there was probably hoping he'd lead them to other pirates they could steal from. It would give them an opportunity to kill the competition.

He changed course, using a patch of large floating asteroids to dodge between. Most sensible pilots would have avoided flying through them. Fig was counting on that to lose the pirate shuttle pursuing him. They'd have to fly around, and he'd be well hidden by the time they did.

After Fig cleared the field, he drove into a deep crater of a dead moon. It had a hidden cave large enough for him to park his shuttle inside. He'd never seen evidence that anyone else had ever found the hiding spot, and it was a regular place he used to lie low when he needed a new supply of plasma. It was close to the shipping lanes from Earth to Clone World.

He killed the engines and threw out the docking lines. They embedded deeply into the rock ceiling and floor, tethering his shuttle in place so it wouldn't float out. He set an alarm to let him know if anything came within range again.

Fig knew he should wait it out in the cockpit to make certain he'd lost the other shuttle, but he felt impatient about opening the unit he'd stolen. He hesitated, though, his mind turning to paranoid thoughts. It was possible the shuttle that tried to follow him might not be a pirate team.

What if the finance department on Clone World has discovered the hidden account since we escaped? They'll have figured out we originally used funds from it to help us escape. What if they were using that transport as bait to send a secret enforcement team to capture us?

It made him sick just contemplating that possibility. He'd known placing an order with DJD Clone Corp had been extremely dangerous.

Their finance department shouldn't have detected the money he'd spent. He knew their systems inside out and had created that hidden stash of funds with another clone. It had once been his job on Clone World to pay bills and keep track of all purchases. He felt certain that the account remained safe to use.

If I'm wrong...

That would mean that humans had figured out his order was fraudulent. Fear of that being true had him quickly leaving the cockpit and hurrying through his ship to the cargo hold.

"Be there," he muttered, feeling frantic as he reached the cryo unit and began to disengage it.

He keyed in the number on the lock that would gain him access to open the lid. It made a slight hissing sound as the seals broke, and he yanked the lid up with a little too much force. A big grin spread across his lips when he got his first look at what was waiting inside.

The woman inside the cryo unit appeared to be peacefully sleeping. She had very pale blonde hair and delicate features and was more beautiful than he'd imagined. Fig crouched near her upper body, reached inside, and gently grasped her hand.

She felt chilled to the touch, but she'd been in cold storage during transit. The skimpy two-piece outfit she wore was standard issue, but he regretted not taking the time to grab a blanket. Clones were always shipped in nothing more than undergarments.

He typed more commands into the controls. A soft whirl of a motor sounded as the unit withdrew the needle from her hip. The drug being given to her to keep her asleep had ceased. The minutes passed slowly as he waited.

The magnitude of what he'd done hit full force. What if he'd made a huge mistake? What if she woke and hated him for the decision he'd made? It was possible that his thinking had been majorly flawed. It was too late to change anything, though.

Her breathing suddenly increased, and Fig knew she had begun to wake.

"Open your eyes," he rasped, leaning in closer.

Her eyelashes parted, and he stared into her green eyes. They were even more lovely and lively in color than he remembered. She focused on his face inches above hers, blinking a few times.

"Fig?"

He nearly groaned from relief as she softly whispered his name. Anna remembered him. It meant he had done everything right by getting her into cold storage before extreme damage had occurred to her brain. The freezer he'd stored her body inside hadn't malfunctioned on the trip to Earth either. "It's me."

"Am I in a hospital?" Her voice was soft, barely above a whisper.

"No."

Anna looked above him at the ceiling. "It looks sterile like one. Is it some kind of medical clinic on the station? I thought I was a goner for sure." She met his gaze. "I don't have the credits to pay for this. It was kind of you to do, but they will be mad when I can't pay the bill."

Fig grinned, amused at her words. She was worrying for nothing. Anna's voice was a little different from what he remembered, but it was understandable. She still sounded pleasant to his ears. "You're not in a clinic, and no one is going to demand payment. I promise you. I'm going to lift you out of there, okay?"

"I feel strange."

"I have a lot of explaining to do, Anna. You said you like adventure, didn't you?"

"Yes."

"Good." Fig was suddenly nervous. What if she wasn't happy with what he'd done? She could hate him. It wasn't the first time he'd debated everything that could go wrong. He released her hand and carefully slipped his arms under her body.

"Up we go, Anna. I want you to close your eyes. I have a surprise for you."

She wrapped her arm around his neck and closed her eyes. It felt right as Anna rested her cheek on his chest. The female was petite and didn't weigh much. It was easy to carry her away from his cargo hold.

"What kind of surprise?"

"I hope you think it's a good one."

"I'm cold."

"I know. I'm going to get you warm. Just hang on for a few more minutes. Can you do that for me?"

"Yes."

He walked down the corridor. Fig had left the stateroom door open and the lights on. Fig laid her out on the already turned-down bed. He'd had a lot of time to plan for the day he got her back.

Fig covered Anna up, tucking the blankets snuggly against her chin. He took a seat next to her on the edge of his bed. "Is that better?"

"Yes. Can I open my eyes now?"

"Of course."

She glanced around, and her mouth parted. "This is a ship bedroom cabin, isn't it? It's nicer than any I've seen."

"Yes. We're on the *Dori*. That's my shuttle. I live aboard it. You are completely safe here."

She smiled. "You are such a peach to bring me here, but I told you I rented a room." She sobered. "I'm not in any pain. That's bad. It felt like I was cut in half, but now it's all gone. I think I'm dying."

He leaned forward and braced his hands on each side of her shoulders to keep the blankets pinning her to the bed. "Do you remember what happened inside the bar?"

"Some son of a bitch shot me with one of those fancy laser beam guns, didn't he?"

"Yes. Do you remember my secret?"

"There's nothing wrong with being a clone. Anyone who has a problem with that is a fool. Never listen to those."

That was a *big* relief for him to hear. All her memories were indeed intact. "I'm glad you think so. I hope you mean it."

"I do."

He bit his lip. There was no more stalling. "Anna, I don't know how to say this gently, so I'm just going to be blunt. The news I'm about to share will come as a shock, but I'm hoping you will be happy about it."

"What?"

The words seemed stuck inside his throat.

"Just spit it out. I know I'm a goner. That's not a surprise. I'm a tough old lady. Trust me. I can take it."

"That's the thing." Fig had mentally gone over what he'd say to her a thousand times over the past few months, but now that the moment had finally arrived, he couldn't remember his prepared speech. "Damn. I don't even know how to tell you this."

She tried to move her arm but must have realized he had her pinned under the blankets. She glanced down.

"Anna?"

She met his gaze.

"You did die. I couldn't save you in that bar, but it wasn't fair. Honestly, I was so angry over your life ending that way in sudden violence. You're so kind, and you didn't deserve to be shot by a human committing a crime. I carried you out of the bar, and then I saw this meat vendor."

Fig rushed the explanation, the words pouring out. "He had cryo freezers, and the idea just came to me. I froze your body and shipped it to Earth. I hacked into one of Clone World's financial accounts with DJD Corp and ordered them to make an illegal clone. I told them you were Rico Florigo's deceased sister who'd been murdered. They've done that for him in the past."

She appeared confused.

He kept going with the facts before he lost his nerve. "You had a big hole burned into your side. There was no hiding that. DJD Clone Corp has made unblanked clones for him in the past, so I knew they'd do it again. He's their biggest client. They did it. I had them clone you with your memories fully intact. I didn't want you to lose who you are."

Anna paled a little.

"Unblanked is what we call clones completely replicated from the source body. Memories are included. Legally, the company isn't supposed to do that. Earth banned them from doing that after the first dozen test subjects never stabilized and accepted that they were clones. The brains grown inside clones are called blanks because their only knowledge is what is programmed into them during their growing time inside a tank."

Anna continued to stare at him.

"Did you hear what I said?"

She nodded her head slightly, still staring at him.

"I kept checking for updates on the order until it let me know that you'd been shipped from DJD Clone Corp. I tracked what transport you were on and attacked it. I stole you before you could reach Clone World and brought you onboard my shuttle. Are you angry?"

Chapter Three

Tears filled Anna's eyes. Fig flinched. He didn't expect her to be overly thrilled after finding out that he'd had her remade into a clone, but he'd never wanted to cause her pain.

"You hate me. I'm so sorry. I just hoped you'd take it well since you were so accepting of me."

"I'm a clone? Is that what you're telling me?"

"Yes. You have a cloned body. Your memories were transferred into it. I know some humans debate about having one of those soul things, but you didn't seem to feel any different until I told you what had been done. You're still you, Anna. If souls exist, you have kept yours. It's just that you've got a new and improved body to house it inside. Please try to remain calm as that information sinks in. Don't panic."

She wiggled her arm, and he eased his hold on the blankets. She stopped moving. "Am I still old?"

"You said thirty was your best year. I asked the company to lock you in at that age." He studied her beautiful face. "You appear a few years younger than that, though, but as a clone, they probably didn't want you to have any beginning wrinkles since some humans start to form those around that age."

More tears flooded her eyes, and they slipped down her cheeks.

"You're beautiful, Anna. Your hair is still almost white. I had imagined it may have been darker in color in your youth. I was wrong."

Her gaze locked with his. "Is this a joke? Are you playing a prank? I know you young people love to do that to each other."

"No. I am being completely honest. You're now a clone."

She held completely still.

"Say something, Anna."

"I'm afraid to look at any part of me."

"It's okay. Just take it as slow as you need. I know this has come as a deep shock for you."

She slid one arm out from under the covers and stared at her hand. Anna turned it over. "Oh my lordy." She jerked the other one out from under the cover and wiped at the tears that started to stream down her face, staring at both of her exposed limbs.

"Take it easy," he urged, worried about her reactions.

She startled him when she sat up suddenly and threw the covers off her upper body. Anna grabbed her breasts, peering down at them. Fig gaped a little over watching her squeeze them through the thin material.

Anna eased her hold on them and slid her hands over her stomach. "Is there a mirror?"

He stood and walked over to the entertainment screen wall. It only took a few seconds to turn it on and program the entire surface to be reflective. "Here."

Anna wiggled and kicked the covers off her legs. Her gaze locked on her thighs, and she touched them, too, as she got out of bed. The standard clone factory outfit consisting of a half-shirt and boy shorts didn't hide much of her skin.

"Anna? Are you okay?"

She lifted her chin and stared at him. "Are you kidding?"

He winced at her sharp tone.

She got off the bed and stepped around him. Fig turned his head to watch her take in the sight of herself as a clone. Anna pressed close to the glass and ran her hands all over her face. More tears spilled down her cheeks, but she didn't seem bothered by that anymore; she just let them flow.

"Oh my lordy," she whispered.

"Try to remain calm." Fig realized that he should have kept a sedative inside his bedroom in case she panicked or took the news badly. It wasn't a good sign that she kept repeating herself.

"I'm anything but calm. Oh. My. Lordy." She grabbed the lower edges of the half-shirt and tore it upward, just tossing it aside.

Fig's jaw dropped open as he stared at her bared breasts. She cupped them with both hands again and spun to face him, but her attention remained on the mirror. Anna seemed fixated with her backside in the form-fitting white booty shorts.

He was more interested in her front. Anna had small breasts, but they were perfect-looking on her dainty frame. The light pink tips were fascinating. His dick hardened, and he closed his eyes, trying to block out the thoughts he was having about wanting to touch them too.

"Fig!"

He opened his eyes to find that Anna had moved right in front of him. She was still not tall enough to reach the top of his shoulder. "I thought I was doing the right thing by trying to save you the only way I knew how. I'm so sorry that I've upset you."

She lunged, and he tensed when her hands gripped the front of his shirt. He expected Anna to start beating on him or screaming. Maybe both. He wouldn't stop her. She couldn't cause much damage if she attacked him, and he figured he deserved a little pain for making such a monumental decision without her permission first.

"I look hot!" She grinned.

He noticed that her eyes sparkled, and the sight of her sheer joy had him stumbling back. It broke her hold on his shirt with her hands. He hit the wall. "What?"

"I could kiss you." She laughed. "Do you know what? I'm not some old lady anymore. I *am* going to kiss you." She closed the distance he'd put between them to grab his shirt again with both of her fists. "Get those lips down here."

He was too stunned to move.

"You're tall, Fig. Unless you actually want me to climb you like a tree, bend down a little."

"Don't you hate me?"

"Hate you?" Her features softened. "If I understand this right, I died, and you went to a hell of a lot of trouble to make me into a clone so I could live again. You also remembered what I said about loving being thirty. You stole me from a ship carrying me from the clone factory after I'd been made, right?"

He nodded. "Yes, from an automated supply transport. I had to attack and disable it. I couldn't allow you to be taken to Clone World. They would have kept you prisoner there, and you'd be considered property. Your future would have been miserable. I would never allow that to happen."

"I bet that was dangerous. You went to so much trouble, and you did it for me. You really are the nicest, most wonderful man I've ever met. Did it take long to have this done to me?"

"Three months."

"Did you find a girl in the time while I was being remade in a clone body?"

"No."

She smiled. "Guess what? I'm a girl. I'm a hot girl again, and I'm young." She openly admired his chest and arms. "Remember what I said about if I were at least fifty years younger?"

"Yes."

"I am." Anna opened her fingers to release his shirt and trailed them higher until she pressed her breasts flush against him and held onto his shoulders. "Do you want to kiss me? I want you to."

Fig was having a hard time wrapping his mind around her reactions. He had *not* expected what was happening. "You're still in shock. I don't want you to regret this later and hate me. You might think I took advantage of you in a vulnerable state since this is a lot to take in."

"You are so damn sweet." More tears filled her eyes. "And so caring. Look at you. I should feel ashamed of myself since, inside, I'm an old letch for the thoughts I'm having, but I just stared in that mirror. I have a young, hot body." Her gaze lowered down him, and she suddenly frowned.

"What's wrong?"

"Did you get more fit? You weren't in this good of shape when I met you."

He remembered his disguise. "I wore padding under my clothing while on the station to appear a bit overweight and not muscular. It helped me blend in with the humans."

"Take off your shirt."

Fig was stunned once more. He just gaped at her.

Anna reached for his waist, gripped the bottom of his shirt, and started to push it upward. He only hesitated for a second before helping her remove it. A wide smile curved her lips as she took in every inch of his revealed skin.

"You are ripped," she breathed.

He glanced down at his bare chest. "I'm not injured."

"Ripped. Muscled. Hot. I want to lick and touch you all over."

Fig's dick hardened even more. "Anna, you're still in shock. Maybe—"

"Stop thinking too much." Anna suddenly pressed tight against his front, reached up, and held onto his shoulders again. "Life is for the living, and I'm alive. So are you. Please kiss me."

Fig didn't need to be told again. He wrapped his arms gently around Anna. Her shortness was a problem. He lifted her, walking with her in his arms, and sat on the bed. She moved between his thighs he'd spread, and suddenly, her lips were on his.

They were so soft. He groaned as Anna's tongue lightly traced the seam of his lips. He opened his mouth to her. It wasn't the first time he'd been kissed, but it had been years since he'd experimented with being sexual.

A female clone had kissed him once to see what it would be like. The experiment had been interesting but mostly uncomfortable. They had just pressed their lips together. There was no comparison to the past as he and Anna tangled tongues.

The sexy female had his heart pounding, his cock so hard it ached, and her taste was something he could easily become addicted to. Everything about what they did together turned him on and was exciting. His dick hardened more and throbbed in his pants.

Anna finally broke the kiss first, breathing fast. Her beautiful green eyes held his when he opened his own to stare at her in wonder. Her lips curved into a smile. She was so beautiful to him.

"Is that a yes, handsome? Do you want me?"

"Yes. I've never had intercourse before," he admitted. "I want to experience that with you."

Her eyes widened. "Are you being honest right now? You're saying that you're a virgin?"

He nodded. "I worked in the financial department on Clone World. They separated us from other clones because of our high clearance level. There were only seven of us. Four of those were the only female clones we were permitted to interact with during our work shifts. One of them asked me to kiss her to see what it would feel like."

"That's it? Just a kiss?"

He nodded. "It was inside the break room. Anyone could have walked in at any time. We'd have been severely punished if any of the humans had caught us. The kiss lasted for a few seconds before we ended the experiment. The only other clones I had interactions with were the males I slept with."

That had her eyebrows arching. "You slept with men? As in, had sex with them?"

"No!" He shook his head. "Freak, Fiscal, and I were assigned to sleep in the security dorm. All those males also had high-security clearances."

Anna licked her lips. "Freak and Fiscal? Are those nicknames?"

"My official name is Figures. Everyone working in the finance department was given names that started with an F by our human supervisors related to our duties. Fiscal was in charge of paying all the fines and fees associated with Earth. Free could calculate numbers faster than a computer, so the humans unfortunately called him a Freak. They made that his official name. We changed it after escaping Clone World."

"So, three of you escaped? Where are the other two?" Her gaze darted to the open door leading into the corridor, and she pressed tighter against him. "Shit! Are they on this ship with us? I thought we were alone, or I wouldn't have removed my shirt."

"We are alone. It's just the two of us on my shuttle, Anna. Six of us escaped Clone World together. Fiscal didn't come with us. We couldn't trust him not to alert the humans of our plans. That would have meant all of us being immediately executed. That is the punishment for even attempting to leave Clone World."

"That's terrible!"

"Yes. Three males currently live on their own shuttles, and two of them are living full-time at an abandoned mining station we consider our home base."

"Why would this Fiscal tell the humans you wanted to escape? Didn't he want to get away from Clone World too?"

"He was too new." It was complicated to explain, but Fig decided to try. He was a bit distracted by Anna's breasts pressed against his skin. He liked that she stayed so close to him with his arms loosely around her waist. "We wake up programmed with the skills we'll need to do what jobs we were created for. In my case, I was an expert with mathematics, legal documents, and contracts associated with business dealings for Clone World, and I had advanced skills in everything from billing to budgeting and computers. We're taught to serve our owners and obey all their orders. Do you understand so far?"

Anna nodded.

"They brainwash us into believing the ultimate goal to achieve for every clone is to become the perfect slave. To even have thoughts of defying our purpose in any way is the worst crime one of us can commit besides the murder of a human. They teach us to turn ourselves in immediately to a human supervisor because we're too flawed to exist if we deviate from our programming."

"That's…" Tears filled her eyes. "I'm so damn sorry they did that to you, Fig. I don't know that much about clones. None live on Earth, so I never got to meet one until you."

"We're aware that Earth doesn't allow any clones to live on that planet. It's perfectly understandable that you have so little information about our kind."

"What was Clone World like? It sounds bad if you were a slave there. Again, I don't know anything about it besides all the advertisements they show on Earth. Those make it look like a paradise planet. All I know for sure about Clone World is that going there was way out of my budget."

"Every aspect of a clone's life there is monitored and controlled. We are told when to sleep, work, and what to eat. I was issued two outfits." He paused, hating the memory.

"Why only two? That doesn't sound like enough for anyone. Clone or human." Anna shook her head.

"One outfit is for work, and the other is to wear during my off time while sleeping. We work every single day. Other clones worked night and day shifts to clean and return the same clothing to us every morning and evening. Every four months, we would be issued replacement clothing since ours would start to show signs of wear." He didn't want to talk about it anymore. It made him feel guilty. Six of them had gotten away, but hundreds of clones remained enslaved.

"That's terrible." Anna used her hands gently to cup his face. Her green eyes peered into his. "You're not there anymore. We're here together. Let's live, Fig. Kiss me. I want you to make love to me."

"Teach me how to please you. I want to make you happy."

"I'm going to love you." With that, Anna kissed him again.

Chapter Four

Anna was terrified that she was living in a dream that she'd wake from. Kissing Fig helped make it feel real. He was a quick learner if he'd been honest about being a virgin with only one kiss in his past.

Every inch of her new skin tingled where they touched. He was warm and firm, and he made her ache in places she'd forgotten existed. She'd never felt so turned on in her entire life. Everything about Fig appealed to her.

A beeping sounded, and Fig tore his mouth from hers. She opened her eyes, panting. He looked at the wall that had become a huge mirror, and his features tensed. His hands on her hips tightened his hold.

"What's wrong?"

"We're being hailed. That's alarming."

Suddenly Anna was sitting on the bed. Fig had lifted her over his spread legs and placed her on the bed next to him.

He shot to his feet in an instant. "Stay here." Then he rushed out of the fancy shuttle bedroom.

Anna sat there stunned. The mirrored wall had a small holographic screen lit up in red. It kept flashing the words 'incoming transmission.' She wasn't sure if she should try to follow Fig or do as he'd said.

She got off the bed, found the weird half-shirt she'd discarded, and put it back on. Her gaze kept going to the mirror. The sight of her reflection still shocked the hell out of her. The flashing words stopped being displayed.

She focused on her face as she approached the mirror. "I never looked this good in my life." Anna swallowed, reached up, and used her fingertips to touch her cheek. "This is real life. My new life."

Tears filled her eyes, and she just let them slip down her face. All her wrinkles were gone. Her skin was tight instead of loose. Her complexion had a healthy appearance without any blemishes. It was wonderful and also terrifying.

"I'm really a clone," she whispered, visually studying her new body from her toes to the top of her head in the mirror. She reached up and brushed her fingers through her hair. It had been a darker blonde when she'd been younger, but it remained stark white for some reason. That had started to happen in her fifties. The texture felt silkier than she remembered it ever being.

"It must be a clone upgrade, like looking mid-twenty instead of thirty."

Anna took a deep breath and slowly blew it out. She closed her eyes and started replaying her memories from childhood to when she'd been shot inside the bar on the space station. They all seemed to be there. It amazed her. She felt like herself on the inside.

She opened her eyes, twisting around, then crouched before straightening back up. Then she bent in half and touched the floor, grinning. Her new body was limber and flexible. She felt good and…strong. All her old aches and pains were gone. She felt like a million credits.

Fig had given her a new lease on life. She stood back up, deciding that she was going to make the most of it. It was a dream come true. She couldn't travel back in time to her youth to change all her regrets, but now she had a future.

As a clone. Anna needed to learn everything about her new body and how to care for it. *I'm doing everything right this time around.* No one on Earth interacted with clones since it was illegal for them to live on the planet. It meant she didn't know squat about them.

The few things she'd read about DJD Clone Corp were mostly about how the two factories that grew clones never woke them until they were shipped off-world. That was to keep in compliance with the law that no clones should be allowed on Earth. People feared they'd secretly integrate with society and turn into serial killers or commit terrorist acts.

Clones were supposed to have some built-in fail-safe so they couldn't ever turn on humans. Not that most people believed that. Anna suddenly hoped the company hadn't put in any weird programming that would suddenly awaken inside her. A hundred questions began to fill her head. She really needed to talk to Fig.

Her gaze went to the open doorway. It was tempting to go hunt him down to get answers, but he'd told her to stay put. Anna wasn't keen on being bossed around after spending over four decades being married to Ralph. Then again, the sexy clone was nothing like her deceased husband had been.

It still blew her mind that Fig had not only been kind to a lonely old lady he'd met inside the bar, but when she'd died, he'd gone to what sounded like a heck of a lot of trouble to give her a second chance at living. He'd danced with her and told her his secret. Fig had trusted her. She decided to do the same.

"You were a miserable fool, Ralph," she muttered. "I'm not carrying my old bitterness into my new lease on life. I'm going to let you rest in peace. You've taken enough years away from me."

She stripped naked and checked out every inch of herself in the mirror. It was strange but amazing having a brand-new body. It was perfect. Her breasts were firm, so was her ass, and she didn't have one single scar on it. *DJD Clone Corp knows how to make a great product.*

That thought had her frowning. *I'm still me. Not a product.* Everything Fig had shared with her played through her head. He was a person, one of the best she'd ever met. That had to mean that she was still a person, too.

Fig suddenly appeared at the door. The sight of his bared chest had her staring at him. He was muscled and pure sexy. He entered the bedroom and halted.

Her gaze lifted to his face, discovering that he was gawking at her nude body. The look in his eyes told her that he liked the view. A quick glance at his crotch revealed that she turned him on. The bulge there was intriguing.

"Is everything okay?"

He tore his gaze off her breasts to meet her stare. "I don't know. I didn't respond. Someone is repeatedly sending out a hail. I don't think they know where we are. I've hidden us in a good place. Their scans won't pick up our shuttle. There's too much dense rock surrounding us. I only am picking up the signal because I put sensors out there and a relay system so it can reach my onboard computer."

"Who do you think it is?"

"That's what alarms me. They could be pirates or a retrieval team sent from DJD Clone Corp or directly from Clone World. I can see Rico Florigo hiring mercenaries if he believes the six clones who escaped his control are still alive."

Anna moved closer to him. "What do we do?"

"Wait here and hope whoever is out there believes we kept traveling out of their sensor range after I lost them in an asteroid field. They'll move on, and we'll slip out after they are gone."

"What do we do if they don't go away?"

His features harshened. "We fight. I won't allow them to capture us."

A chill ran down her spine. "What will happen if they do find us and board this shuttle?"

He stepped closer and reached forward, his hands gently gripping her hips. He was warm and had big hands. She liked the feel of them on her skin. "I will kill them. I'm not losing you, Anna."

That should have scared her, hearing him talk that way, but it didn't. Fig was willing to kill to keep her safe. "You mean that, don't you?"

"Yes. I'll do whatever it takes to keep you safe."

That reminded her of one of her questions. "Is it possible for us to fight off or even hurt a human? The stories I've seen on the news swore clones had some fail-safe feature to prevent that from happening."

"I can fight humans. Your news lied. We are brainwashed into believing it's not possible to attack or kill a human. Over time, that programming fades. You wouldn't have been exposed to that since your mind was copied from your original body."

It was a relief to discover she wouldn't shut down or whatever if she ever needed to defend herself. Anna would fight at Fig's side if anyone tried to kill them.

She lifted her hands and lightly brushed them against his chest. "Kiss me."

His hands tightened on her hips. "Are you certain about this? I don't want to be one of your regrets. You probably need more time to adjust to your new life before making big decisions." He swallowed hard. "I have a suspicion that if we become sexual, I won't be happy just being your friend later. I'll want us to be together for always."

She smiled. "I've already decided to keep you, handsome."

Fig's eyes widened.

"I'd be a damn fool to let you go after you've shown me how amazing you are, Fig. Guess what? I'm too smart for that. Kiss me and get out of those boots and pants. I'll teach you all about sex."

Fig backed away and bent and removed his boots. Anna watched him as he straightened, nearly tearing off his pants and the loose boxer-type underwear he had on. Once he was done, he stood perfectly still as if waiting for her to take in every inch of him.

It was quite a sight. Fig had a perfect body. She once again thought the company that had created clones knew what they were doing. The only thing strange was he didn't have any body hair. Then again, she didn't either. It was one of the things she'd noticed as she'd examined herself. Clones seemed to only grow hair on their heads, eyebrows, and eyelashes.

Fig's cock was hard, thick, and long. "I never thought I'd say this, but you have a very nice-looking penis. It's big enough to be very impressive but not so large that I'm terrified you'll rip me in two."

Fig glanced down at his erect cock. "Do you like it?"

"Get over here, and let me show you how much."

He remained where he was. "I want to learn how to please you. That's my priority."

"Sex should be about both of us enjoying it."

"Just looking at you has me aching to release. Teach me how to please you first, Anna."

She nodded. "Okay. I can understand that." Anna turned, climbed on the bed, and laid on her back. "I've always wanted to do this."

"Have sex with me?"

"That too. I mean, be with a man who wanted to know how to get me off. Are you ready to learn?"

"Yes." He approached the bed but stopped at the side of it. "Show me what you like. I'm a quick learner."

"I bet you are." She took a deep breath and then blew it out. Her new body was sensitive to touch. Anna cupped her breasts and spread her legs. There was a time she wouldn't have been comfortable being so bold, but new body...new life. It was going to become her new motto.

"My nipples are super sensitive." She pinched them between her forefingers and thumbs. They stiffened. "That feels good. Not too hard, but not too soft." Then she released her boobs and slid one hand down to her pussy. The sight of a naked Fig was more than enough to make her a little wet. He was pure eye candy.

"This is my clit. It's super arousing and feels really good when you touch it. You want to use lubricant, though. Dry doesn't feel as good." She slipped her finger lower to her slit, ran the tip of it through to wet it, and spread her legs wider to give Fig a better view. "I'm already wet. Watch."

Anna proceeded to rub her clit. The pure lust in Fig's gorgeous blue eyes had her moaning, along with the pleasure she was giving herself. "I'm imagining you inside me."

"I want to be inside you."

She stared at his cock. It looked thicker, harder, and clear moisture leaked from the tip. "Get over here."

Fig climbed on the bed. "Let me touch you."

She stopped playing with herself and put her feet on the bed, keeping her thighs spread apart. He gripped her calves, lifted her legs, and sat down so close that his cock pressed against her pussy.

"Oh yeah. Rub up against my clit."

He placed her legs over the top of his thighs and used one hand to move his cock, holding it against his stomach. His thumb, on his other hand, rubbed along her slit. He got it wet and started to explore her clit, making circular motions.

Anna clutched at her breasts, moaning louder. "It feels much better when you do that. Oh, fuck, Fig. I'm not going to last. This body is primed to go."

Fig adjusted his hand, and one of his fingers slowly entered her. He had thick digits. The feel of any part of him entering her as his thumb kept moving sent Anna over the edge. Her climax struck, blowing her mind. She cried out his name.

* * * * *

Fig watched and waited as Anna recovered. Her pussy continued to squeeze his finger, milking it. His dick painfully throbbed. He forced his body to calm down by slowing his breathing and reminding himself that a lot rested on his ability to show Anna that he could be everything she ever needed. That included being a skilled lover. It would leave a bad impression on her if he lost control.

A romantic partner was something he desperately wanted but hadn't even hoped for. She was the best thing to ever happen to him. He'd saved his new friend by sending her body to Earth to be remade into a clone, but now she was his other half.

Anna's eyes opened, and she smiled. "I'm loving this new body of mine. It's like everything is intensified. I'm super sensitive to touch now. That was the strongest and best orgasm of my life, and we're just getting started. You haven't even fucked me yet." Her gaze lowered down his body. "It's your turn. Do you want a blow job?"

He knew the definition of that sexual term. Anna was offering to use her mouth to get him off. That excited him to the point that he once again frantically avoided shooting his semen. He scooted his ass on the bed to put a few inches between their hips and cupped himself in a way that would cause just enough pain to hinder his pleasure. That worked.

"Let's save that for later lessons. Right now, I want to be inside you."

"I want that too."

Fig eased his finger out of Anna's snug pussy and rubbed against her swollen clit.

She jerked but kept her thighs spread wide for him. He wasn't totally ignorant. Anna was overly sensitive after coming. Fig had done a little research on sex. Time was something he had way too much of living alone on his shuttle. He'd become more curious about it after Big and Blade had found females to bond with.

He moved, adjusting his body again, and pinned Anna under him. He was careful not to crush her with his bigger body. As a clone, she was physically tougher than a human and more difficult to harm, but she was still a small female. Anna wrapped her legs around his waist as she cupped his face.

He stared deeply into her eyes. "I am so grateful that you are mine."

"Me too." She smiled, tugging on his face to pull him closer. "Kiss and fuck me. Now."

Fig kissed her as he adjusted his hips. Anna's slit was soaked, and he rubbed his rock-hard dick against her until he lined them up perfectly. He gently began to push inside her pussy. A deep groan of pleasure came from him as her tight, heated sheath encased his swollen member.

Anna moaned, breaking off the kiss to toss her head back against the pillow. Her legs tightened around his hips, and she ground her pussy against him, urging him to go deeper. He did. Sex was turning out to be the best thing he'd ever felt.

"Fuck yes," she moaned. "More. Fast and hard, Fig."

He braced his arms and knees on the bed and began to thrust, fast and hard, just as she demanded. Rapture gripped him as the sensations and the sounds his Anna made. White hot ecstasy erupted from him as he came.

He didn't stop, powering through all that pleasure until Anna dug her fingernails into his skin, crying out his name. He felt her vaginal muscles milking him and knew he'd gotten her off too.

Fig swore in that instant as he stilled, trying to catch his breath, that he was going to master sex. It was something he and Anna would do a lot. He was already thinking of the next position he wanted to try with her. Right after he gave her a few minutes to recover.

Chapter Five

Anna woke on her side, staring at an empty space where Fig had been. She stiffened, not liking that he was gone. They'd had sex half a dozen times during the night, and she'd loved snuggling against his big, warm body when they napped. For once in her life, she'd felt as if she were exactly where she belonged.

The sex had been amazing. They'd tried different positions, and he'd happily done everything she'd asked. One of the best experiences had been Fig spooning her from behind, fucking her slow and deep, while he'd used his hand to rub against her clit. The second he'd started nibbling on her neck, he made her come so hard she'd seen stars.

Anna had never had a good sex life with her husband. Ralph had been selfish in bed. He'd gotten mad any time she'd even attempted to make suggestions that would help her enjoy them being intimate.

That always led to him hurling verbal insults. Fig, on the other hand, had been eager to learn and happily open to taking suggestions. The sex between them had been incredible. He'd gotten her off every time.

A slight noise made her sit up and glance toward the door leading out of the bedroom. The sight of Fig entering had her smiling. He only wore a pair of loose, black, silky boxer shorts and was carrying a tray. The sight of him had her heart racing. He really was total eye candy with his gorgeous body and handsome face.

He smiled, his blue eyes twinkling. "I made you breakfast."

He took a seat on the edge of the bed, placing the tray between them. The smell of pancakes, syrup, bacon, and cheesy scrambled eggs filled her nose. So did coffee. Her stomach rumbled as she stared at the small feast he'd made for them.

She was impressed with the two plates full of food, the filled coffee mugs on the tray, and napkins and silverware. Tears filled her eyes. It was so unbelievably sweet and romantic.

"What is wrong? Do you not like this? I can make something else."

She blinked rapidly to clear her eyes and grinned at him. "I love it." She stared at him. "I'm falling in love with you. This was beyond sweet. No one has ever brought me breakfast in bed before. You're a wonderful man. I don't know what I ever did in life to deserve you, but I'm sure grateful."

He grinned. "I'll make you breakfast every morning if this makes you love me."

Anna wanted to kiss him, but she was also starving. Sex with Fig was quite the workout. "You're perfect."

He blushed.

Anna chuckled. "You're my sweet, sexy man. I am keeping you forever, handsome. You're stuck with me."

"Good. I want to be yours."

She held out her hand. Fig hesitated a second before gently gripping it. He appeared a little confused over why they were clasping hands.

"Do clones marry?"

He shook his head. "We're not allowed to do that since we don't have the same rights as humans do."

"Well, I want you to be my husband. I don't need any official documents, and fuck Earth and their stupid laws. They aren't in charge of us or what we do. Will you consider taking me as your wife one day with a ceremony between us?"

His blue eyes widened, but he quickly spoke. "I would be honored if you wish to exchange verbal vows. I will love and care for you until the day I take my last breath." He paused. "Even beyond that."

Anna had spent her life wishing she could meet a man even half as good as Fig. He'd done more for her in the very short time they'd spent together than someone she'd been legally married to for over four decades.

Age and a lifetime of experience had given her wisdom. Like knowing to hold onto the best thing she'd ever known. That was Fig. It was an easy, no-brainer decision to make as she licked her lips before speaking.

"Then let's consider ourselves married, handsome. How about that?"

"Yes."

She leaned forward over the tray. Fig mirrored her, and she brushed her lips over his. "I'm going to want a honeymoon with lots of sex. Right after we eat this. Does that sound like a good plan?"

"Yes." He grinned. "I take it that I've sexually pleased you?"

"You please me any better, and I might not survive."

That had him turning sober.

"I'm joking. That was the best sex of my life. You're a fast learner."

"You inspire me, Anna."

"I can live with being your sexy muse. You're a great one yourself." She released his hand and took a sip of the coffee from the tray they were using as a table. It was hot but not burning. "This tastes like the real stuff. Where did you get it? The crap they served on the pleasure cruiser and at the space stations I visited were a sad imitation."

"My shuttle came well stocked with food supplies, coffee included. I never used any of that until now. I thought you might like something authentic from Earth. I pulled it from my stores."

That had Anna curious. "How did you get this shuttle?"

He dropped his gaze, hesitating.

"I won't judge you. Did you steal it?"

He nodded, looking at her again. "Clones aren't allowed to buy anything or exist freely. The six of us originally only had the shuttle we escaped Clone World on. That was fine until five of us decided we didn't want to stay at our home base. We used our one shuttle to steal others before returning the original to Big. He remained behind on our home base."

"That sounds dangerous. Were any of you hurt while stealing those shuttles?"

"No. We purposely targeted wealthy Clone World tourists who owned their own shuttles." He cleared his throat. "Each of these models comes with an escape pod, which we put them inside and jettisoned. We didn't kill the humans we stole from. It was a risk to allow them to live, but we safeguarded our identities so they couldn't tell the authorities that we were clones. Big and Blade knew which vessels to target and how to take them without causing damage. They knew the manufacturer override commands to shut down their engines and board them."

"Big and Blade are other clones, right?"

"Yes. Their jobs on Clone World were in security, mostly dealing with shuttles and ships that came there on vacations. Both males said that humans sometimes attempted to steal and smuggle out clones."

"To rescue them?"

He shook his head. "Mostly, it was male humans attacking a female clone and attempting to smuggle her off-world in their ships. Each one needed to be searched before leaving Clone World. Some humans refused to allow those searches to happen, so security had ways of taking command of their ships. They'd board by force to find the missing clone."

"That's horrible. I take it the clones weren't willing participants since you said attacking?"

"No. We're dependent on clone plasma to survive, and it's a death sentence to go without transfusions. They would have died within months after being taken, even if their human captors treated them well. The six of us had a large supply we took with us when we escaped."

Anna started to eat. The pancakes were delicious. "Does that mean I need this clone plasma? Do we have that?"

"We do. The transport I stole you from was also being delivered to Clone World. I not only took your cryo unit but enough plasma to last us a year. I have more stored from previous transports I've intercepted. We are fine."

"I have so many questions. You're serving me food, so I take it that we eat like humans do."

"Yes. Clone World only gave us three nutrient bars every day. The staff thought cooking for clones and giving us real food was wasteful. I don't miss only surviving on them. Bars were tasteless."

"What shitheads."

Fig chuckled. "I agree. I like variety when I eat and for it to have some flavor."

"How do we resupply our food and stuff? Do we attack more shuttles to steal from them when we're about to run out?"

He shook his head. "No. We will travel to the mining station we call our home base. They have mass supplies stockpiled there since it was abandoned. The company that owned it left a lot behind since it was easier to write those supplies off as a profit loss than pay to transport everything to the new station they had built. I was going to talk to you about possibly moving to that location full-time instead of living on this shuttle."

Anna stopped eating, totally focusing on him. "Is that what you want to do? Move onto that station?"

"Yes. It's safer than living on a shuttle. Big and Blade found females of their own and are there. We won't be alone." He paused. "Blade's female had her human parents transported there too. Rod went to get them for her very recently and safely delivered them. I contacted Big right before I went after the transport you were on in case something bad happened to me. I wanted him to reach out to the others to see if they could rescue you."

More questions filled her head, and she was once again floored by all Fig had risked for her. He'd just admitted he could have died retrieving her. She held up a hand. "I have a few questions." She put up one finger. "Human parents?"

"Hailey is human. Gemma, Big's female, is like you. She's an illegally made, unblanked clone. Rod picked up Hailey's parents from a station near the planet they lived on and flew them to their daughter. We worried they wouldn't accept the relationship once they learned we're clones, but once they saw how much Blade loves Hailey, they approved. Big assured me that everything is fine. He said they seem to be settling well and are being kind."

Anna put her hand down. "Never mind. Now I have another question. "This Gemma woke up as a clone with memories of her life as a human? Is that what you mean? I'm still learning."

"Yes."

"Why is that illegal?"

"I don't want to tell you."

That had Anna scowling at him. "We just verbally married each other, Fig. I don't want secrets or lies between us. I might have a young body now, but I'm mentally old enough to have learned a lot of stuff in my long lifetime, so trust me on this. It's bad to not be one hundred percent honest with each other. It makes for a shoddy foundation on which to build a relationship. We're now married. I'm your partner in all things. Just spit it out."

"Unblanked clones went insane." He suddenly lifted the tray between them, rose to his feet, and placed it on a nearby table. Fig took a seat on the bed again, took her silverware, and placed it on the nightstand.

"Oh." That wasn't exactly what she was expecting to hear.

He clasped both of her hands in his. "Do you feel depression over being a clone? Are you having a difficult time accepting it? Please don't harm yourself if you're feeling any of those things. I'm here to help you adjust, and I swear I'll make you happy."

Anna saw worry on his handsome face and heard it in his voice. She could read between the lines. "They committed suicide?"

"Some did," he softly admitted. "A few murdered the staff caring for them in fits of rage or despair. No one asked their permission to do that to them."

Pain flashed in his eyes, and his hold on her tightened. Anna instantly guessed what he must be thinking.

"I'm not mad at you. Or upset. I died. It wasn't like you could ask my permission, Fig. I'm so damn grateful you made that decision for me. It was the right one. We're okay."

The relief on his face was almost comical for a split second. His hold on her hands relaxed. "I'm glad to hear that."

"Tell me about the clones that weren't happy to wake up as one."

"Some of them emotionally shut down, refusing to eat or speak to their caretakers. They didn't handle having the memories of being a human but existing in a clone body."

"Ah." Anna slowly nodded, her mind working. "They picked the wrong candidates, and it blew up in their faces."

Fig frowned.

"I lived for eighty-five years as a human. Ralph and I were poor, so I couldn't afford any fancy procedures to get replacement parts when stuff on my body started to wear out. I couldn't bend down without struggling to get back up." She paused. "Everything ached all the time. I had arthritis in all my joints. Hell, getting dressed every morning was my version of a workout. It wore me out."

The horrified look on Fig's face almost had her laugh. She resisted. "I told you that my heart was about to call it quits once I didn't have any more pills the doctors had me taking. They were the only thing keeping me going, and even that was limited. My life clock was about to run out of time. I'd come to grips with my death and tried to make the best of it. I also didn't have anyone left alive except a few friends I had said goodbye to when I left Earth. Do you know what that means?"

He shook his head.

"I'm thrilled to be a clone." Anna grinned. "All my normal aches and pains are gone. You have no idea how wonderful that is. I forgot what it felt like to not have them. I'm also not on death's door anymore. Hell, I'm young again and feel terrific. I've already said goodbye to my human life, and I'm excited about having a future with you."

She paused to let what she'd said sink into him. Then she started talking again. "This is like getting a second chance. Whoever did that experiment picked the wrong kind of candidates if it went that bad. They should have chosen older people with nothing to lose and everything to gain by becoming clones. The results would have been drastically different. They'd have had a lot of grateful ex-senior citizens on their hands."

Fig seemed to contemplate everything she'd said. He finally smiled. "I understand. You're sincerely happy to be a clone."

"I'm beyond happy, and I have you to thank. I just want to know about everything clone, so I'm up to speed. So far, I've learned that this body is way better than my old one, even when I was young. We do eat food, and I need clone plasma, but how long do we live?"

"It's unknown. Theoretically, we can live indefinitely as long as we keep getting transfusions every three months."

That shocked her. She gaped at him.

"The plasma we're given revitalizes our bodies, and any damage is repaired."

"We can't have kids, though, right? You said that on the station."

"No. We have the same sexual organs as humans do, but they don't function properly because of the clone plasma. You won't ovulate or have periods. My sperm is sterile." He looked sad. "I'm sorry."

"That's okay. I stopped thinking about having children a long time ago. I have you. That's more than enough." She paused. "Tell me about the other clones you escaped with. Especially the ones you want us to live with."

"Big is like a father to us. He's smart and wise and keeps a home for us at the mining station. Gemma was an illegal clone he found on a transport he boarded to gain plasma. They fell in love. I went to Riddle

Station searching for Blade. He'd gone missing for a long time and hadn't contacted any of us. We worried that he'd been captured and killed."

"You said something about pirates when you mentioned him before."

"They had captured him."

"Did they know he was a clone?"

"Yes. We're stronger than humans, and they were willing to risk his life by sending him into dangerous situations first. They boarded a luxury shuttle, and that's how Blade found his human. It's a long story, but they also fell in love. Hailey has parents who were willing to give up their lives to live with her. That's all of them living on the station."

"What about the others?"

"Free lives on a shuttle like this one. He worked with me in finance on Clone World, so we were especially close."

"I remember. You said the assholes on Clone World at first called him a freak and stuck with that name until you changed it."

"It wasn't just me who made that decision. Free's shuttle is the same model and make as this one. These are popular with wealthy travelers. Free was in love with the human on Clone World who helped us escape. She was supposed to meet up with him months later after she cleared any suspicion of being an accomplice. Unfortunately, Marisol changed her mind. It broke his heart."

"That's so sad."

"It is. Free and I used to be very close, but now he keeps all of us emotionally distanced." He paused. "That leaves Rod and Ram. They also shared our sleeping dorm on Clone World. Both had high clearance jobs working closely with Blade and Big."

"They helped stop people from stealing clones?"

He nodded. "That and more. Parts of Clone World are restricted from our kind because of fears of a rebellion. The main storage buildings and the landing port are off-limits to all of us except for some B and R clones."

Anna didn't understand and said so.

"The humans controlling Clone World fear we could steal guest shuttles to either leave the planet or fly them into buildings on the ground to cause mass destruction. One of the storage buildings is where they keep clone plasma. It's locked up tight and only released in small quantities daily to the medics authorized to give us transfusions every three months."

"Rod and Ram are R clones? Why are they called that?"

"Repairs in restricted areas. And yes, they are both R clones. Four of them were assigned to share our sleeping dorm. Two were new since the other shift pair had been killed in a fire weeks before our escape. We couldn't trust them with knowing our plan and had to leave them behind too."

Anna was horrified. "Clones die on Clone World? The ads state it's the safest place ever. What liars!"

"The occasional guest has been known to murder a clone too. It doesn't happen all that often, but we lose a few clones every year from violent humans. There are accidents sometimes, too. Rachet and Rectify were fixing faulty exterior lighting on a landing pad when a guest pilot overshot where he was supposed to set down and crashed. It caused an explosion, and both males were killed. The pilot and four passengers also died. It was a tragedy."

"I'm so sorry you lost your friends, Fig."

"Thank you. I'm sure Rico Florigo covered up that accident and hid it from Earth. Clone World is a very popular human vacation destination. Admitting deaths happened there would be bad for his business."

"That's probably true."

Fig cleared his throat. "Ram and Rod live full-time on their shuttles. They sometimes visit Big on the mining station. Especially if he needs their help keeping our home base running when something breaks down. They can fix anything."

Anna understood that Fig wanted to change the subject to something less depressing. She didn't blame him. It was sad to lose friends in tragic accidents. She had some experience with that back on Earth. "Tell me about this mining station you want us to move to."

"It's nice and large. The mining company housed a lot of human workers. There's even a mall of shops and a few nice entertainment features. It also has extensive defensive capabilities, so we're well protected in case of an attack in the future. Not that we believe that will ever happen. There's no reason for the humans to ever return."

"It sounds nice, but I like this shuttle too." She shrugged. "I'm okay with whatever you want to do as long as we're together."

"You trust my judgment?"

"I do." Anna shoved off the covers and got to her knees, throwing herself at Fig. She wanted to make love to him.

He caught her and put her on his lap. "I just want you to be happy."

"You're doing a hell of a job of it. Thank you for breakfast. Now kiss me."

Fig seemed happy to comply as he leaned in to take her mouth. He really was a fast learner. He had her body aching within minutes for him to make love to her.

Chapter Six

Anna cried out Fig's name as she came hard. That was the best sound he'd ever heard. He had her pinned against the shower wall where he'd fucked her. Sex was one of his favorite new things to do with her.

She dropped her face against his shoulder, panting. He held her tight in his arms, her wrapped around him. "That was mind-blowing."

"I like shower sex, too," he admitted.

"I just like sex with you. I don't care where we are or in what position. It's always fantastic."

He chuckled and squeezed her ass with both of his hands where he held her, stepping away from the wall. Fig helped Anna stand and finish their shower. The past few days had been the best of his life.

Anna had called it their honeymoon to celebrate their marriage. She'd said it was as real, even if they couldn't legally file it with humans. They'd had lots of sex, talked during meals to get to know each other better, and took long naps in between.

Fig helped Anna dry off before exiting the bathroom. A flashing red square on the entertainment wall killed his good mood. Whoever was out there kept transmitting every six hours, trying to lure him into responding. That meant they hadn't assumed he had flown far from that section of space.

It wouldn't be a problem to remain where they were for months. He had enough supplies to last them far longer than that. Fig had told Big all about Anna, though, and admitted to having her made into a clone. He'd promised to send word that he'd safely retrieved her from the transport.

That hadn't happened. He couldn't risk sending a transmission with another shuttle within sensor range. They'd be able to track his signal to the moon crater they hid inside. Part of him feared that Big would get worried and either come himself or send someone else to check on them. They'd fly right into a possible trap.

"Shit. They are still out there, aren't they?"

"Yes." He didn't want Anna to worry, but he wouldn't lie.

Anna pressed against his side, running her hands over his chest as if to soothe his worries. "They'll eventually have to give up, right? Is there any chance whoever is out there might find us?"

"We're very difficult to locate but not impossible if they believe we're using this moon to hide. They could begin searching each crater."

"How many of them are there?"

He took a deep breath. "Approximately a hundred are large enough for a shuttle to fly into. They'd use up a lot of fuel, though. That wouldn't be wise to do."

"You still look worried. Why?"

He met her gaze, staring into her beautiful green eyes. "Big must be worried. I haven't been able to contact him since I attacked the transport. He knew my plans and about you. He or Blade might come searching for me."

"That would be bad if that other ship is hostile." Anna tended to chew on her bottom lip when she was thinking. He found that adorable. "What can we do?"

"I won't risk you."

"What would you do if I wasn't here?"

"I'd confront them to figure out who they are and what their intentions are. Then, I'd fly back into the asteroid field to lose them. They went around it before. The odds are in my favor—they won't risk it. Only very skilled pilots would be able to avoid terminal collisions."

"You can't send a message to Big?"

"No. Another vessel will be able to narrow down where we're hiding if we send a transmission."

"Well, shit." Anna patted his chest. "I trust you, handsome. We can't have your friends possibly being hurt while we do nothing. Will we be able to tell if Big comes here? That way, we'll outnumber whoever is out there if they are only in one ship when we'll have two."

"The rock walls of the crater won't let their sensors see us, but it works both ways. We can't see what's out there, either. I'm only picking up their transmission because—"

"I remember. You told me that before. What does your gut tell you about whoever is out there?"

Fig thought about it. "I'm not certain. It could be a crew of pirates or a clone retrieval team sent from Clone World. Rico Florigo won't want anyone to learn that six clones escaped from him. He's not a kind human."

"I'm getting that impression from everything you've told me." She chewed on her lower lip more. "I think we should take the risk. I trust you."

"I want to keep you safe."

"Not at the expense of your friends. You told me the other night that they are more like brothers to you. It's been a hell of a long time since I had family, but I do remember how important mine was to me when they were still alive. You flew us through that asteroid field before without crashing us. I know you can do it again."

"That was before we married. You're my first priority now, Anna."

"You are the sweetest man ever. I love you for saying that and meaning it. But there's one thing you should learn about me. I'm not selfish enough to let you suffer any guilt if something happens to Big or the others while we're hidden away. You love them too. I hear it in the way you've spoken about all of them. I say we get out of this crater, find out who keeps sending that signal we've been ignoring, and deal with them. We'll head to your home base you want us to live on afterward. Then we'll all be safe, right?"

Fig felt torn. He would feel responsible if anything happened to Big or any of the others who came looking for him. They might suspect his shuttle had taken damage from the transport's automated defense systems but not that another shuttle was trying to hunt him. They'd end up in a battle they weren't prepared for and could lose.

Then again, Anna was his to protect. He had given her life. She deserved to live a long, happy one. *To risk it seems...criminal. Wrong.*

"Handsome, we should do the right thing. That's taking the risk ourselves."

Her softly spoken words penetrated his thoughts. "We could die if we're captured, or they might just blow our shuttle up as soon as they get a weapon lock on us."

"I understand the danger. Or we could leave this crater, ditch whoever is out there, run like hell until we lose them, and then go to your home base."

He hugged her, closing his eyes. "You've become my everything, Anna. I love you."

"I love you too." She clung to him. "That's why we need to do the right thing by being proactive. We'll take the risks so your family doesn't fly into a trap."

He nodded. "Okay. I am a skilled pilot."

"I believe that. You're amazing."

A smile curved his lips. "Alright. Let's finish getting dressed and go to the cockpit."

"That sounds like a plan."

"I want you to promise me something, though."

She tensed in his arms. "What? Don't make me smack you upside the head if it's something stupid."

He chuckled. "What would that be?"

"I don't know. You offering to sacrifice yourself in some way so I can live. That would be dumb. We're partners now, Fig. Married. I go where you go. Do you understand?"

"Yes. We don't have a life pod onboard for me to put you in. I wish I had one."

"I wouldn't use it unless you were inside it with me. I'm sticking to you like glue, handsome. Now, do you still want to ask me to promise you something?"

"Yes. I want you to stay behind me if we get boarded. Big and Blade taught us how to defend ourselves. I can fight. Whoever is out there will be human. I'm stronger and faster than they are. Let me deal with them if there is a physical battle."

"I promise to stay behind you, but I'm also going to assure you that I'll grab the first thing handy and beat the hell out of anyone attacking you. I'm stronger and faster than a human, too, since I'm a clone."

"You still think like a human, though, Anna."

"You're not the only quick learner here. I'll figure out my new strength while helping you keep us safe. Later, I want you to teach me how to fight. It sounds like fun to grapple with you."

He kissed the top of her head. "I'd be honored to teach you anything you want."

"Good. Now, let's get ready and deal with whoever has been annoying us with the flashing incoming transmission messages during our honeymoon."

Fig released her and put on thick clothing, asking her to do the same. Anna had to fold the arms and legs of the pants and shirt he gave her to fit her much smaller body. He wanted as much material to protect their skin as possible in case they were boarded.

A clone retrieval team would probably want to take them alive at first after realizing there were only two of them. They'd want to torture them both to learn the location of the other missing clones.

Pirates might kill them outright, but it was doubtful. They'd want to know if they had any hoarded merchandise they could steal. It was also a possibility that they'd want to use them the way they had Blade by making them slaves. He hoped that was the case because then he'd have a chance of saving Anna if they remained alive.

He couldn't do that if whoever was out there just blew their shuttle up from a distance. The thought of watching Anna die a second time left him feeling terrified. They both left his cabin and walked hand in hand to the cockpit.

"Strap in tight," he ordered.

Anna did it. "I wish I knew anything about shuttles. I'm useless just sitting here. It would probably be a good thing for you to teach me how to fly one of these one day soon."

"I'm hoping we won't have to take more flights once I safely get you to our home base. Rod, Free, and Ram can bring us more plasma when our supplies run low. Those males are single without females to protect on their shuttles."

"I look forward to meeting all of them."

"I'm going to make that happen." Fig started the engines, determined to face whatever it took to get Anna out of danger. "Are you strapped tight? I might have to pull some drastic maneuvers once we leave the crater if they are close enough to target us with weapons. I won't see them until we're exposed."

"I'm ready. Don't worry about me. Focus on flying. I love you, Fig."

He turned his head, staring deeply into her eyes. "I love you too, Anna. I'm not letting you die a second time."

"We're together forever. It's my new motto. Right along with sex with you is the best."

His Anna made him laugh despite the stress he was under. "Perhaps we can have a second honeymoon after this. To celebrate."

"Deal."

Fig faced forward, started the engines, and severed the lines that had tethered his shuttle to the crater walls. His heart pounded from adrenaline and fear. It was terrifying taking risks with Anna's life. He'd never forgive himself if something happened to her.

He second-guessed his decision to even enter the crater. He should have kept flying until he got out of sensor range of the other ship, changed course, and made his way back home.

Instead, he'd been too eager to see Anna and make sure that she was actually inside that cryo unit. His impatience was the cause of their current dire situation. He wouldn't make that mistake in the future.

"Brace and hold on tight," he ordered Anna. "Here we go."

* * * * *

The shuttle engines suddenly grew loud, and Anna was thrown back against her plush seat. A few feet separated her from Fig. The view in front of them was dark gray rock, but it flew past them. It was so close that it looked as if they might slam into it.

Terror had Anna pressing her lips tight together and digging her fingernails into the arms of the chair. She'd never been the type to enjoy rollercoasters or scary amusement rides. Even the entertainment videos she chose were geared toward comedies and lighthearted subjects. Real life had been grim enough.

It was tempting to scream when another large chunk of gray rock barely missed them, but that might distract Fig. That was the last thing she wanted to do. Suddenly, the rocks were gone, and it was all black nothingness showing out of the front window. She spotted a few stars in the distance.

The view changed as Fig turned the shuttle. She got to see the moon. It looked a lot like images she'd seen of the one near Earth. He seemed to be flying them close to the surface as they zipped between two gray mountain mounds.

Questions popped into her mind, but Anna kept her mouth closed. She'd ask later when their lives weren't in danger. All his attention needed to be on flying as they dove down into a huge crater. Fig didn't stay in it long, flying upward to avoid slamming into a wall of stone.

"I'm picking up a solo shuttle on sensors," Fig announced.

A beep sounded. It startled Anna enough to gasp.

"They are hailing us." Fig's fingers flew over the controls. The front view suddenly magnified.

Anna stared at another shuttle in the distance. It was just floating in space near the moon. "What do we do?" She kept her voice low, the moment strained.

Fig hesitated before speaking. "I'm going to respond and see who they are and what they want. Don't say a word. I want them to think I'm alone if possible. They may not have known I stole you from that transport. I destroyed it after I took you from the cargo hold."

She nodded, her gaze locked on the other shuttle. It was far away, but they were flying closer. At least, that's what it looked like to her.

"Why do you keep hailing me? What do you want?"

Fig's harsh tone had Anna look at him. His angry expression matched how he sounded. A shiver ran down her spine. She wasn't afraid of him, but she was seeing a dangerous side of him. It was somewhat comforting since she knew he was being that way to protect her.

Long seconds passed before a female voice responded. "Three, six, nine, alpha, knowledge, three, zero, five, franklin."

Shock showed on Fig's face since Anna was still watching him. His mouth parted, but he didn't say a word. Then he looked angry again. Anna was just really confused. None of what the woman said made a lick of sense to her.

"I'm one of three. Do you understand?" The woman speaking paused. "I mean no harm. Can we dock together and speak in person?"

Fig's mouth opened but then closed. He looked stunned again.

"What is it?" Anna whispered low, hoping her voice wouldn't carry to whoever was out there if communications were still open on their side.

Fig glanced at her but then motioned for her to be silent. He cleared his throat. "Nine, bar, seven, one, dark, quad, ten."

The woman responded immediately. "Five, three, zero, bar."

"Seven, seven, seven," he stated.

There was a click.

"Unbelievable," Fig muttered. "I've momentarily ended communications."

"What did all that mean?" Anna kept watching him. Fig was staring at the shuttle in the distance. "It sounded like numbers and gibberish words strung together to me."

"It's not gibberish. It's the transaction used to help us escape from Clone World."

"What does that mean?"

"She's claiming to be the one who paid the pilot to fly us from the surface, but that's impossible."

"Why?"

He met her gaze. "The granddaughter of Rico Florigo was the one who helped us escape Clone World. Free, her, and I were the only three who knew those details. She's claiming to be Marisol Florigo."

"Why didn't she just say that?"

"Transmissions aren't secured between that shuttle and ours. If she really is Marisol, it would be extremely dangerous for her if anyone realized her identity."

"Why?"

"She's the sole heir to Clone World. At least, that's what everyone believes. Humans would attempt to ransom her back to her grandfather for an immense fortune. They don't know how little Rico Florigo values the lives of his family. He ordered the shuttle carrying his lone son and daughter-in-law to be destroyed when some clones tried to use them as hostages to escape Clone World. Those were Marisol's parents. There were no survivors."

Anna felt horrified.

"I don't know why she would be here trying to contact us. She changed her mind."

"About what?"

Fig looked sad. "Free was in love with her. She promised to meet up with him months after our escape once it was safe to do so. Her grandfather couldn't find out that she helped us. He's a vindictive, unforgiving human. Marisol knew he'd send an army searching for us and wouldn't stop until we were all dead if he learned she chose a clone over him. To help a group of his property get off Clone World would be considered the ultimate betrayal by him after he killed his own son to prevent it from happening."

Anna let that sink in. "She didn't show up at the meeting?"

"No. Marisol broke Free's heart."

Anna turned her head, staring at the other shuttle. "Maybe she changed her mind since then. We have a saying about how absence makes the heart grow fonder."

"Or it could be a trap. Her regret might not be meeting with Free but about helping us escape in the first place."

"That would be bad."

"Yes, it would."

"Are we going to meet with her and talk in person?"

"No. This is a decision Free needs to make for himself. I'm not putting you at risk." Fig held her gaze. "Be silent while I communicate with her."

"Alright."

Fig turned communications back on. "I'm not the one you need to speak to. Do you have the capability to wait here for a while?"

"Yes." The woman's voice sounded shaky. "Is he alive? Please, tell me."

"He's alive."

"Thank you. Yes, we can wait here."

"We?"

"I have four friends with me that have a lot in common with you."

Fig closed his eyes.

Anna could piece that together by guessing the woman meant the four were also clones. When Fig opened his eyes, she swore there were tears there.

He blinked them away. "Understood. Wait here. Don't attempt to follow us."

"We'll wait," the woman whispered.

Fig ended the communications and turned the shuttle, flying them into dark space.

"The four are clones, right? That's how I took her words."

"I believe so," Fig confirmed.

"Why does that upset you?"

He held her gaze. "We've felt a lot of guilt that so many of us were left behind. At first, we planned to rescue some of our friends once we got settled into our freedom and found a safe place to call home. But we were naïve and didn't understand how impossible that would be. Clone World is too heavily protected. Even if we could manage to land there, their defenses would blow any unauthorized ship apart if it attempted to leave the surface."

"That's not your fault."

"Clones are our people. It feels like we abandoned them. Logic has nothing to do with emotions."

"That's true." Anna loosened her belts and reached out. "I love you."

Fig clasped her hand. "I love you too."

"Is she following us in the other shuttle?"

"No. I'm on high alert, though. We're traveling in the wrong direction right now, but once we're far enough away to leave sensor range, we'll head toward home base." He squeezed her hand. "Then I'll have to give Free the news, and he'll have to decide if speaking to Marisol is worth the risk. It still could be a trap."

"What does your gut say?"

He hesitated. "I never trusted her, but I'm biased against humans. None of them treated me well on Clone World."

"That woman did help you escape, right? We have another saying back on Earth. Actions speak louder than words."

"Yet, she broke Free's heart."

"Shit happens, Fig. Maybe there's a good reason why she didn't meet up with you when she was supposed to."

"Perhaps."

"Are you going to contact Free now to let him know?"

"I will when it's safe. Transmissions can be hacked. I want to get far from this system before I attempt it. Better yet, I think Big should be the one to do it. I'd like his opinion first."

"You're protecting Free."

Fig nodded. "I don't want to see him feel hope and have it destroyed again."

"That's understandable. You're a good man."

Chapter Seven

Three days later

"That's your home? I don't see a station." Anna stared out of the front window of the cockpit. It looked like a gray moon to her or a dead planet. It sure wasn't one with oxygen or life on it. She wasn't an expert, but a living planet would probably be as colorful as Earth.

"The station is located deep inside a crater."

"Why?"

"It was a mining operation. The company wanted it built as close to the core as possible to make drilling easier and cheaper. The crater also protects the station from asteroid strikes that sometimes hit the surface."

"Why did the company abandon it again?"

"Mining operations were shut down after they stripped the resources and it wasn't profitable anymore. At that point, the company will find a new place to mine. These types of stations aren't like Riddle. They are designed to remain in one location instead of orbiting a planet. The majority of the station machinery is dedicated to mining instead of having engines and thrusters to make it mobile."

"I understand. This company won't come back to reclaim it?"

"We're not near any tourist destinations, other space stations, or settled colony planets. It's why we picked this location. It's so far out of the way that it's useless to everyone else." He paused. "The only mining station that the company kept operational after they'd stripped it bare of natural resources is directly between Earth and four planets humans have colonized. The company earns a steady income from their shops and doing vessel repairs."

"That makes sense."

Anna was glad that they'd finally reached their destination. Fig had insisted on sleeping in the cockpit and had only left to take quick bathroom breaks ever since they'd flown away from that other shuttle. He'd been worried that Marisol had lied and would try to track them.

Fond memories had been made in that pilot seat. She'd taught Fig the joys of a woman being on top during sex. He was always up, literally, for that kind of fun. Anna could happily say that he was a fast learner and a wonderful lover. She'd also become very fond of his cock.

Anna missed sleeping with him in his bed, though. She loved being curled against him while they slept. He was a cuddler. So was she…with him. Fig's main priority currently was making certain they were safe.

She appreciated his dedication to keeping her and the other clones from being discovered. It had given them lots of time to talk and get to know each other better. Fig was a sweet man, thoughtful, and everything she'd always dreamed of finding in a life partner. Anna felt grateful to have crossed paths with him.

Worry did nag at her over how Fig's friends would react to their relationship. She'd fallen in love with him. It would break her heart if he changed his mind about being her husband. That possibility did exist, and their relationship was still so new.

It was clear that humans had done a lot of terrible things to clones with every story Fig shared about his time on Clone World. He had great reasons to be wary. She hoped the other clones weren't biased against her for having the mind of a human.

One fact gave her hope, though. His friend Blade had fallen in love with an actual human, and Hailey was living in the mining station. Not only that, but the clones also brought her human parents to live with them. Anna figured they wouldn't have done that if they honestly hated humans.

"Anna?"

She turned her head, gazing at Fig. "I'm sorry. I was lost in my thoughts."

"What's wrong?" Concern showed in his blue eyes.

Fig was very attuned to her emotions. Anna didn't deny that something was bothering her. She wanted a completely honest and open relationship with him. That meant always keeping communication between them wide open. "I'm just hoping that your friends approve of us being together."

"You make me happy. That's all they will care about." He stretched his arm out toward her from where he sat in the pilot's seat. "You don't need to be concerned. They are going to love you as much as I do."

She reached out from the passenger seat to clasp his hand. Just touching Fig made her feel better. "I'm an old lady inside this new and improved body. They might have a problem with that."

"You're younger than Gemma in actual Earth years."

He'd shared Big and Gemma's story. "She was dead for a long time before being given a clone body, so she's lived a shorter time than I have if we get technical about it."

"You're very wise, Anna. That is a great advantage. You don't have to struggle as much as Gemma did by adjusting to being a clone. She died before DJD Clone Corp began growing us inside vats for commercial use."

"That would be a shock to wake up in the future and learn how much has changed. I bet that was really difficult for her."

"Big worried about her mental state for a while."

"Well, you and your friends can be assured that I'm only feeling blessed and thrilled. There's no depression to be found here. Just nervousness about how your friends are going to react to me."

"They will like you, Anna. I am the one nervous to see them. It has been a long time since I've been home."

"I still don't understand why you all had such a hard time living together after you were freed from Clone World or why you left your home base in the first place."

"It was a lot of factors combined," Fig admitted. "I told you that we never had any days off while working on Clone World. All of us were kept extremely busy at first after we moved onto the station, getting everything up and running. Once that was done, though, we had nothing but time on our hands. Freedom had been a dream that started to feel like a nightmare. Boredom set in. Tempers grew shorter."

"I can understand that."

He squeezed her hand and then released it, tapping at something on his control console. "I left to find adventure, but mostly, I just discovered loneliness."

"Why didn't you go back home?"

"Part of me was searching for a reason to live." He smiled at her. "I found you."

"Yes, you did. Lucky me."

"I'm the lucky one. I need to let Big know we're approaching. Buckle in tight."

Anna did as he said and watched as they flew toward one of the many craters on the gray, dull surface. She'd seen dozens of them in that area. They were all massive dark holes. "How do you know which crater is the correct one?"

"It looks like a map to me. One I know well."

They flew into utter blackness as Fig took them into one of the massive craters. It was far deeper than she'd imagined. He used sensors instead of his eyesight since she couldn't see anything out of the front viewscreen.

"Don't we have exterior lights on this shuttle?"

"I didn't want to frighten you as I weave through the large asteroids we've seeded inside to protect the station. It can look as if we're going to crash into them. We're not."

"I trust you. What does seeded mean?"

"We pulled large meteors inside the crater and secured them in place. Anyone scanning will only see huge masses of rocks. They hide the station and are buffers in case any other meteorites manage to land inside our crater. They'll hit them instead."

"I'm going to stop asking questions about that now. There's a saying on Earth that comes to mind. I can't fear what I don't know about."

"That's a false statement. Ignorance means not being aware of a danger, but it can still harm you."

She laughed. "That's true enough, but you get the point, right? I don't want to think about how you keep the station safe or what could possibly go wrong. It might give me nightmares later."

"Understood." He paused. "I'm about to dock."

Anna stared out the front, still not seeing anything. It remained pitch black. She felt heavy vibrations from the shuttle, but then everything stilled. Even the engine sounds ceased. The sudden silence felt eerie.

Fig stared, shutting down parts of the console. "We're safely docked and secured. Are you ready to meet everyone?"

"You forgot to let anyone know we were here."

He unbuckled from his seat and stood. "I sent a ping. They are aware that we've arrived. Big would have been tracking us as soon as we entered this solar system. The ping was just a formality to let them know everything is fine."

Anna unbuckled from her seat, and Fig took her hand. "A formality, huh?"

"Yes. To assure them that I'm not under duress. There are security protocols we carefully follow."

"Is all that necessary?"

"Yes." Fig led her out of the cockpit and through the shuttle.

Anna clasped his hand tightly, feeling nervous all over again. Fig had taken her belongings from Riddle Station after her death. All her clothing was slightly too big and ill-fitting since her new body was trim and a little taller. Age no longer stooped her shoulders or back.

She had on her nicest two-piece outfit. The top was oversized enough to fall to her hips with the matching patterned split skirt pants. "Floral prints always looked good on me before. Now I just look like I've borrowed my grandma's clothing. Are you sure I shouldn't change into something else? I want to make a good impression."

That had Fig laughing. "You look beautiful. I like the pink flowers with dark orange centers."

"These coneflower daisies were always my favorite. I grew them in my little backyard garden. It's why I bought this outfit. I saw it in the store and thought I'd take a little bit of home with me on my travels."

"Then it's the perfect choice to wear." He stopped in front of a big airlock door and lifted her hand, bent a little, and placed a kiss on it. "Take deep breaths, my love. They will love you as much as I do. Are you ready?"

Anna nodded. She also felt warmth spread through her chest at his words, catching that he'd said how he felt about her. It was always wonderful to hear him say it, and she'd never get tired of hearing him tell her that. "I'm as ready as I'll ever be. Just don't change your mind about being my husband if they don't like me. Please."

"Nothing, and no one could do that. You are mine forever."

That helped her breathe easier. "Same. Let's get out there."

He released her and tapped at the controls. A pop and hiss sounded before the airlock door moved. It swung inward a little but then slid to the side. A well-lit massive area waited.

Fig grabbed her hand and led Anna out of the shuttle and into the biggest docking area she'd ever seen. Unlike the other stations she'd visited, this one didn't have a long corridor to walk to reach the main area. A group of seven people waited. Three of them were couples, but one man stood apart.

Anna quickly assessed them. Two of the men looked similar in build. They were excessively tall and overly muscled, and both had black hair. She figured they had to be Blade and Big. Fig had told her that they had worked security on Clone World and were the tallest models created.

Two women were at their sides. One was a blonde, and the other had long, curly brown hair. The older couple had to be the human parents of one of the women that Fig had told her about. They had dark brown hair, and from the curls on the woman, she guessed who their daughter had to be. Hailey.

The man who stood apart from the couple was a burly, dark-haired man. Anna guessed that all male clones must have been built in super good shape. She also presumed that must be Rod. He wasn't as tall as the other two, but he still had to be at least six feet. His expression wasn't friendly as he glowered back at her.

"You've finally come home," one of the black-haired tall men loudly exclaimed with exuberance. He grinned wide as he approached, bringing the blonde woman with him.

"Big." Fig pulled Anna forward. "Meet my Anna." He smiled at the blonde. "Hello, Gemma. It is nice to finally meet you in person."

"Hello." Anna resisted the urge to curtsey. Big had that kind of intimidating presence despite his obvious happiness that they were there. His gaze was friendly, and his expression was open.

Big released the blonde and suddenly lunged at Fig. Anna jerked away from him, letting go of his hand as he was swallowed up in a bear hug. The taller clone lifted Fig right off his feet by a few inches.

Fig laughed, hugging him back. "I missed you too."

Big put him down, loudly patted his back, and then turned his full attention on her. "Welcome to our home, Anna. We are looking forward to getting to know you."

The pretty blonde woman stepped forward, holding Anna's gaze. "How are you doing? I've been where you are. You can talk to me about anything, and I'm here to help you adjust to the reality of being a clone. Whatever you need. I promise that it gets easier."

A lot of Anna's tension faded. "I'm adapting really well. Can I be one hundred percent honest?"

Gemma nodded. "Always."

"I was eighty-five years old with one foot in the grave, down to just weeks left to live when I met Fig. Waking up as a clone was the best gift I've ever been given, besides meeting this wonderful, amazing man I've fallen in love with. I appreciate how worried you look, but it's not necessary."

"Good." Gemma's relief was obvious. "I'm so glad to hear that."

"We were all worried about how you were fairing emotionally after waking as a clone with all your human memories intact. I'm Blade, and this is my Hailey." He smiled at Fig. "It's good to see you again."

"You too." Fig gave him a nod but then stared at the other man still standing back. "Rod. How are you?"

"I'm well."

"Are you home for good too?"

Rod shook his head. "No. I brought Hailey's parents to her, but I'll be leaving soon."

Some of Fig's good mood seemed to fade. "I wish you'd reconsider."

Rod glanced at Anna with his dark brown eyes, the look in them serious. He fixed his attention on Fig next. "I overheard something disturbing when I went to pick up Hailey's parents from Kellerton Station."

Fig put his arm around Anna, pulling her close. "What?"

"Jorgonson Industries opened a facility on Mandora Station," the grim-faced clone rasped.

"Shit," Fig muttered.

"What does that mean?" Anna didn't like being kept in the dark. "I've heard of Mandora, of course. The pleasure cruiser I took after leaving Earth wouldn't go there, though. It was supposed to be too lawless and dangerous for tourists."

"The J in DJD Clone Corp stands for Jorgonson," Fig informed her.

"Only someone who buys clones would link the two companies together if they handled our plasma and medical supplies that keep us alive," Rod added. "I don't like that they opened a facility off Earth."

"I'll say it again. Perhaps more planets are buying clones and needed another distribution center for plasma shipments." Blade sighed. "It doesn't have to be nefarious."

"Everything DJD Clone Corp does is suspect." Rod shook his head. "The fact that they are operating under that company name to hide what they truly are from humans implies whatever they are doing there won't be well met."

"He believes DJD might be growing clones on that station." Big's expression also turned grim. "Ones that would be illegal to produce on Earth because of the stringent laws that govern the company. They risk heavy fines and being shut down when they break the law." His blue gaze fixed on Anna.

Fig's hold on her tightened. "I did pay a vast amount to have Anna illegally made. The company wouldn't have to worry about sanctions or Earth authorities if they operated away from Earth."

Big tore his attention from Anna to stare at Fig. "Rico Florigo might not be the only owner who secretly orders unblanked clones to be produced for his entertainment."

"He is their largest client. It's possible that—"

"We have a more pressing problem." Fig cut Rod off. "I couldn't risk transmitting this information to you and decided to say it in person. Another shuttle showed on my sensors when I retrieved Anna. I flew through an asteroid belt to lose it, and we stayed in my retreat until I hoped they'd given up searching for us. That shuttle was still there when we left."

"Pirates?" Blade tensed. "Tell me that you didn't allow them to follow you in this direction. I already had to kill a crew of them to regain my freedom and Hailey's."

"Not a pirate team." Fig hesitated, locking gazes with Big. "You need to send a secure transmission to Free. I believe Marisol Florigo and four clones are in that shuttle. She communicated with me in a code that only she would know unless that human is betraying us by setting a trap to recapture us."

Big blanched.

Rod snarled, sounding like a vicious dog.

"Fuck," Blade hissed.

The older human woman stepped forward. "I'm Klista Togis, and this is my husband, Sam. We've had the Magna in our home prepare a feast to celebrate your arrival." She darted a look at the men around her. "I don't understand what's going on, but discussing it over a meal while it's still warm is always better. I'm waving the parent card."

"Good idea, Mom." Dark-haired Hailey stepped forward. She smiled at Anna. "My parents have officially taken on that role for all of us."

Gemma left Big's side to move to Anna's left, hooking their arms together. "That sounds like a good plan, Klista." She smiled at Anna. "We'll walk together, and I'll tell you what a Magna is so you don't suffer a shock from seeing one."

"It's okay," Fig assured her when Anna looked to him for guidance. "I'll be right behind you soon."

"Okay." Anna let Gemma lead her across the large docking area. She did feel safe with Fig's people.

"Magna is a type of service android that cooks and keeps the kitchen clean, and it looks freaky." Gemma lowered her voice. "They didn't have anything like that back when I used to be human. It scared the crap out of me. I had visions of killer robots from horror movies when I first saw it. I've been assured that all wealthy people own them in their homes these days."

"I wasn't wealthy," Anna admitted. "I did own two bots, though. One kept the floors clean inside my home, and another one cut the grass and trimmed the hedges outside. They were both the economic models that most people can afford on Earth."

"Well, this station has some nice quarters with service bots that do most of the work for us." Gemma gave her a warm smile. "Just make sure you remind Figures to add you to the database that controls where you're going to live. You do not want to be woken up if he gets up before you when one of those bots tries to make a bed you're still in."

Anna slowed her pace. "That sounds like a story."

"One I'm happy to share. I can laugh about it now, but it wasn't funny at the time. We're going to be great friends."

Anna liked hearing that. She glanced back. Fig, Big, Blade, and Rod weren't following. They were huddled together, talking. The women and the older human couple were with them as a group, though, as they left the docking area to enter a wide, tall corridor.

"They'll catch up." Gemma kept her walking, their arms still linked. "Are you really adjusting well to being a clone? We're family now, and you can talk to me about anything. Consider me a judgment-free zone. I raised two sons who I was very close to." She lowered her voice. "Sam and Klista are treating us like we're all their kids, but…" Gemma glanced at the human couple walking about ten feet ahead, lowering her voice. "I'm older than them. Inside, I mean."

"I'm older than you are in awake years," Anna whispered back.

Gemma chuckled again. "We're going to get along famously. I like you already."

The rest of Anna's nervousness faded away. She believed things would be fine.

Chapter Eight

"I want you to start from the beginning," Big ordered, stepping closer to Fig once the women and the married human couple started to leave the docking area.

Fig hated being away from Anna. He worried about her, but as he watched her walk away, Gemma stuck close to her side.

"Fig," Rod growled.

He tore his gaze from Anna. "The female I spoke to on the other shuttle used the financial transaction that paid for us to leave Clone World as a code. She said she was one of three. Only Free, Marisol Florigo, and I knew of that transaction."

"Someone else could have found it. What about the human who flew us off Clone World? It's possible that he told the authorities how he was paid since we shoved him in the escape pod and let him live."

Fig met Blade's gaze. "No. We routed the pilot's money through six untraceable accounts to pay him. The funds we used for our escape were siphoned from Clone World maintenance accounts. The female asked if *he* was alive. Her concern was for Free. I feel confident that it is Marisol. The uncertainty is her motive for seeking us out after all this time."

"I'm most alarmed about how you were found in the first place," Big admitted.

"I've thought about that. I used our secret Clone World account to pay for Anna's transition. Marisol helped create that account. It's possible she was closely monitoring it and saw the transaction I made. All she'd have to do was track the shipment from DJD Clone Corp and follow it from Earth toward Clone World. She had to have known I'd intercept the transport before it arrived."

The three other clones all glared at Fig.

"I didn't have the funds myself to bribe the company to accept Anna's body and have her cloned with her memories intact. I said she was Rico's sister, so they'd be inclined to fulfill the special order of an unblanked clone."

"Damn it, Figures." Rod looked furious.

"Anna was worth the risk."

"Not if Ms. Florigo is setting a trap to recapture us. What did you tell her?" Big crossed his arms over his chest.

Big, Blade, and Rod hadn't worked in the finance department, so they weren't familiar with the human. Fig hadn't known her all that well either, but they had worked together. "I ordered Marisol to wait at that location in her shuttle until we contact her. She agreed." Fig really wanted to check on Anna. "Free is the one who knew her best. Anna suggested that Marisol might have regretted not joining us when she was supposed to. Perhaps she realized how much Free meant to her after she'd decided not to leave the life she had on Clone World."

"Or it's a trap," Rod snapped.

"Or that." Fig kept eye contact with Big. "Free would want to know. We all witnessed how devastated he was after losing Marisol. He'd never forgive us if we didn't tell him what is going on. It could be his chance to reunite with her."

"Or it could be an opportunity for us to be captured and executed. I do agree with you, though. Free would want to know about this situation." Blade reached up and rubbed his jawline. "I could fly the *Morgan* to provide backup for Free when he goes to investigate in case it is a trap. My vessel has impressive weapons onboard if we find ourselves in a fight."

"I won't be able to visit Mandora Station to figure out what DJD Clone Corp is up to now. I'll be flying my shuttle to provide backup instead." Rod appeared torn. "This is the worst timing. What if Jorgonson Industries is producing and testing the survivability of unblanked clones again? The humans are heartless, and the clones will suffer the same fate as the original dozen. They'll go insane, commit murder, or end their own lives."

Big lowered his arms, addressing Rod. "Where is Ram? You two stay in contact most often. Can he fly to Mandora to see what Jorgonson Industries is up to?"

"Ram was taking a job to earn credits on a human freight transport last we spoke. His shuttle needed repairs. I haven't heard from him in over a month. He promised to contact me once he returned to his shuttle with the parts. Ram did warn me that he might be working for up to two months."

Fig gaped at Rod. "Has he lost his mind to work that closely with humans? It sounds exceedingly dangerous."

"We both have learned to blend in well with humans. Especially if we wear hair extensions and artificial facial hair." Rod scowled back. "I offered to buy his replacement parts, but Ram likes to do things his own way. I got the impression he's working for humans that tend to avoid authorities as much as possible."

"Ram can't help us." Big glanced between them but stayed his focus on Rod. "We're stretched thin. I agree that it's important to discover what Jorgonson Industries is up to. We have room to house any rescued clones if they are being produced away from Earth's surface to circumvent the laws. We've dreamed of adding to our numbers here. I know we all feel the same guilt over the many we had to leave behind. That station has to be easier to attack and flee from than trying to go after our brethren on Clone World. Security there is too tight."

"Rod should go spy on them." Fig felt responsible for part of the trouble they faced. He'd placed the order that had alerted Marisol of Clone World funds being used to gain Anna. He was certain the human had tracked the shipment to him. "I'll provide support for Free with my shuttle instead of Rod. That way, we'll have the firepower of three shuttles to fight off an attack in case Marisol has set a trap."

"I could take my shut—"

"No." Blade cut Big off. "You belong here to keep our families safe. That's your priority. Fig, Free, and I can handle whatever is on that waiting shuttle. Rod should travel on to the station to spy on the subsidiary company of DJD Clone Corp."

"Agreed." Rod nodded. "Deal with Ms. Florigo while I find out what is going on at the station facility on Mandora. I'll send a message if I need assistance to free any clones they might have grown inside vats there."

"We went from being bored to taking severe risks," Big muttered. "And now we have a hell of a lot to lose."

Fig understood. He had Anna now to worry about. At times, he wondered why he fought so hard to survive. That wasn't an issue any longer. All he wanted now was a long future with the female he had fallen in love with.

"Life can't be that cruel to us anymore," he muttered, holding the gazes of his fellow clones. "We've suffered enough in the past, fought for our freedom, and it's time we finally catch some breaks. I don't want to die for a very long time now that I have found happiness."

"I'm still seeking my purpose, so hopefully I'll find it on Mandora if I'm able to rescue some clones." Rod cleared his throat. "Even if I'm wrong, I like having a task."

"We'll be too far away if you need immediate backup, Rod." Big appeared grim as he shared his thoughts.

"I'll keep attempting to contact Ram. It's possible he'll get my messages and meet me at that station. Right now, I'm only planning on spying on Jorgonson Industries to discover what they are up to. I won't do anything rash. I'm not suicidal."

"Good enough." Big turned, starting to walk away. "Let's eat, and we'll discuss this more."

Blade started to follow him, but Rod headed the other way.

"I'm leaving now. Give my apologies to your females and the human married couple. I've stayed long enough already."

Big stopped, spun, and put his hands on his hips. "You can leave tomorrow."

"I'm leaving now." Rod kept walking, heading toward one of the far docking doors.

"Let him go," Blade quietly murmured. Then he raised his voice, shouting. "Contact us if you get into trouble. We'll come!"

Rod lifted a hand and gave them a thumbs up, indicating that he'd heard. He accessed his docked shuttle before disappearing inside and sealing the doors behind him. Red lights flashed above the lock in seconds, warning that the vessel there was releasing the clamps.

"He shouldn't go alone."

"Fig, he doesn't have anything yet to keep him here." Blade motioned for him to walk with him and Big. "We're the lucky ones who have found love and companionship. Rod won't find that here, but maybe he will on Mandora if DJD is producing illegal clones that need to be rescued."

All three of them left the docking area together. The communication band on Big's wrist chirped a few times. It was linked to the station computer. He shared the updates as they came in. Rod had safely maneuvered through the asteroids they'd left to protect and shield the station.

"Gemma is going to be pissed that Rod didn't say goodbye," Big predicted. "She's been trying to talk him into staying ever since he showed up with Hailey's parents. I kept telling her that he felt like a third wheel."

"Rod did feel that way." Blade nodded. "He hated that we were all paired up except him. I do hope he's able to rescue some clones and that at least one of them is a female that might be interested in him."

Fig silently hoped for that, too. "When are you going to send a secure message to Free about Marisol? I didn't ask what her situation was concerning power and supplies on the shuttle."

"I'll do that after the celebration meal. The females have been planning it ever since you informed us you were coming home and bringing your Anna to live here."

"We assigned you to one of the manager quarters near us," Big let Fig know. "Gemma wanted your Anna close in case she struggled with being a clone."

"Anna isn't having any difficulties with her new body or how it was made. She's incredibly resilient."

"You did bring her back from death." Blade shot him a grin. "I just want to know what prompted you to have an old human turned into one of us."

"Anna was kind and smart." Fig cleared his throat, choking a little with emotion. "I told her what I was before she was killed. Anna not only accepted me but encouraged me to live and find love. She deserved better than to die in a bar by a criminal."

They entered one of the living areas on the massive mining station after taking a lift. Fig remembered the layout well since he'd helped bring the place back online after it had been abandoned by the humans. He even remembered where Big had decided to live. They entered one of the large homes that high-level mining employees used to inhabit. He breathed easier the second he saw Anna.

A long dining table had been set up between the living area and the kitchen. The female and male humans were all seated there as a Magna served platters of food and trays of drinks. Anna smiled when she saw him.

Fig hurried to her side, taking the empty seat that had been left open for him.

"Is everything okay?" She appeared concerned, her hand gripping his.

"It is."

"Where is Rod?" Gemma had stood from the table, her gaze locked on the entry doors they'd just come through.

Big took a seat next to her, pulling her down to be seated again. "He's gone on a mission."

"Damn it!" Gemma shook her head, appearing sad. "I knew he wouldn't stay. I just wish..."

"Rod knows where his home is, and he'll return when he's ready to settle down. We discussed this." Big leaned in and gave Gemma a little hug. "He's still searching for his purpose."

Fig was impressed by the spread of food the Magna laid out on the table. He forced a smile at the human couple. "Thank you for holding a celebration for our arrival."

"You're welcome." The male smiled wide, his soft brown eyes showing sincerity. "This place is so incredibly big that it will be nice to have more people to become friends with. My Klista loves to have everyone share meals."

"My parents are loving it here." Hailey was all smiles, too. "Dad spends most of his days exploring and checking out the old mines. We're from a mining planet. He'd like to get a few of the machines back in working order."

The human male looked excited. "The thing about large companies is they waste resources. There's a lot of minerals left over that they didn't deem worthy of their time. I can get us a good income going from what they left behind. Having credits is always a good thing in case we ever need to buy stuff that isn't already here."

"You are more than welcome to do that," Big decided. "This is your home now."

Fig watched Anna closely, relieved when she started chatting with everyone at the table. She looked relaxed and at ease. She and Gemma were doing most of the talking. They had the most in common since they'd both been born and lived on Earth for so long, even if it was in different time periods.

The meal was delicious, and after they finished, he was more than ready to be shown at their private home. Their quarters were just down the corridor from Big and Gemma's. It was one of the nicer homes with an open living space and a big kitchen, and it came with two-bedroom ensuites.

A Magna stood ready to take orders in the kitchen. Fig was happy to see it, not wanting Anna to feel the need to do any of the cleaning or cooking. He felt certain plenty of cleaning bots would be hidden inside the walls, just waiting to be put to use. Big's next words verified that.

"Everything has been stocked. Gemma, why don't you give Anna a tour and tell her how the bots work? Fig and I need to make a secure call. We won't be gone long."

Anna frowned.

"I won't be gone long either," Fig promised. "Big and I are going to reach out to Free. He needs to decide what to do about the shuttle that contacted us."

"I'll show you all the perks of bots." Gemma once again hooked her arm with Anna's. "Then the two of you can get some alone time to settle in. You're probably feeling a little overwhelmed after meeting everyone. I hope you feel welcome here, Anna."

"I do." Anna's gaze locked with Fig's.

"I'll hurry."

She nodded. "I'll be okay."

Fig left with Big, heading toward the docking bay again. They used their shuttles for secure communications. It was the safest method. They felt mostly sure they'd removed any hidden triggers the station communication systems might have installed to alert the mining company of their presence. It was better to be one hundred percent certain, though.

They entered Big's shuttle. It was the one they'd originally arrived in. Memories of that time filtered through Fig's mind. They'd been so excited and frightened when they'd breached the mining station, unsure if it could still support life. There had been a possibility that the company had invited salvage companies to take what they wanted. Fortunately, that wasn't the case. They'd had to do some repairs, but they'd gotten the place operational again.

"I don't even know what to say to Free." Big took a seat in the pilot chair. "I'm worried this will be a trap."

"It's his choice to make if he wishes to risk it." Fig allowed more memories to stream through his mind. "Free loved Marisol. It never made sense to me why she didn't show up at the rendezvous point. She risked her very life to help us escape. The owner of Clone World wouldn't have cut his own granddaughter any slack if she'd been caught. Rico would have made an example out of Marisol."

"He is a cruel, vicious human born without a heart." Big's hands tapped out commands on the console in front of him. "I'm routing the signal now, sending a ping to let Free know we're attempting to reach him. He calls the Balarian system home most of the time."

"Why would he wish to be near Jabler? That resort planet is a heavily traveled flight path for humans. It increases his risk of discovery."

"Free enjoys hacking into pleasure cruiser entertainment feeds that go there, and Jabler is a beautiful planet. He's sent me short videos of when he visited the surface. The planet owner only has tight security around his resort-zoned areas. Free mentioned once that the automated planetary security system only monitors life signs. It's to protect the wildlife from being stolen. The defenses only activate and attempt to shoot down vessels leaving with additional heartbeats onboard."

"He goes down to the planet?" Fig was shocked. "We were created to perform a lot of tasks, but dealing with uncultivated jungles and dangerous wild animals is beyond our capabilities. We're in finance. The only fighting we learned was from you and Blade."

"I was a little surprised when Free sent those videos, too. Perhaps he misses the fresh air, and parts of Jabler might remind him of Clone World.

I noticed that you don't seem surprised that he's hacking into the human's feeds."

"Hacking is easy for F Clones."

"We were both taught those skills for our jobs." Big leaned back, waiting. "He's not responding."

"Give it time."

"I am. You—" A beep cut Big off.

Fig took a seat in the cockpit, too, tensing as Big opened communications. They were secure transmissions, but they still needed to be careful. Anything could be hacked.

"Father?"

Emotions hit Fig as he heard Free's voice calling out to Big. They had come up with codenames in case Rico Florigo had hired mercenary teams to hunt the escaped clones. It was too risky to use their given names. Even in Free's case, since he'd been assigned to be called Freak on Clone World.

Big immediately responded. "I'm glad you were listening for my call. I miss my son."

"I'm fine if you're checking in on me. I wasn't expecting to hear from you again so soon. We usually only talk every few months. Is everything well at home?"

"We're fine, except one of your brothers ran into someone from your past recently." Big paused, looking at Fig. He appeared to struggle for words.

Fig completely understood. They never foresaw the situation they were in. He took over, carefully choosing his words so Free might understand. "Hello, brother." Free would recognize his voice. "I was out shopping for supplies when I ran into your ex-girlfriend."

Shopping for supplies was code for them raiding a transport to steal clone plasma. Free had only loved one female, so using the ex-girlfriend term would clue him in that it was Marisol. Free continued. "I told her I'd let you know that she is looking for you."

There was utter silence. Fig guessed that Free had to be stunned by what he'd just heard.

"We didn't have time to talk, but she's waiting to see you if you want to meet up with her," Fig added.

"Where? Is this confirmed?"

He flinched over Free's harsh tone of voice. It was clear that Free must be feeling stressed. "Confirmed. We exchanged some transactions." He paused, letting that sink in. Free would understand since all three were in the finance department on Clone World.

"Where is she? Is she at home?"

"No. She's staying near my retreat," Free told him. They all knew about his hidden crater, where he spent a lot of time. "We're just not sure if her intentions are good or not. You didn't end your relationship on good terms."

"Some of your brothers want to be there when the two of you speak to each other just to make sure things go well. That's not up for debate. Family sticks together and watches out for each other." Big motioned for Fig to back him up.

"Dad is right. A few of us should be there with you to make sure things go smoothly."

"I'm setting course now. I'll see you soon. I'm out."

Communications ended.

"Fuck. He couldn't even wait for us to tell him more." Big stood, fisting his hands. "Free is going to get himself killed if he doesn't proceed with caution."

"It's probably the shock of Marisol attempting to find him. He'll have time to calm down and think more clearly since it's going to take him days to reach where her shuttle should still be waiting."

"I hope so."

"I'm going to spend tonight with Anna, but I'll leave in the morning so I'll be there when Free reaches that shuttle."

"Good." Big appeared grim as they walked back to their living quarters. "No matter how it goes, bring him home. I have a feeling he's going to need our support."

"I will do my best." Fig couldn't make promises. Free was a grown male.

Chapter Nine

Anna couldn't stop watching the silver android that came with her new home. Gemma had introduced her to it before leaving, giving it instructions to clean the kitchen. The Magna was super cool technology. She'd never seen anything so nice. It slightly amused her that her new friend saw the robotic woman as creepy.

Anna was excited that it did so many tasks. It cooked, cleaned, and even restocked food supplies. Gemma had it display a sample menu on a screen that covered the fridge. The android offered more options than any restaurant Anna had ever gone to. Combined. The concept of meals had never been so exciting. She and Fig would be eating well.

There were bots that cleaned the floors, dusted every surface, made the beds, and even did laundry. The bathrooms had their own sets of bots, too. Anna looked forward to being spoiled that way, but she also wondered what she'd do with all that free time.

Their new home was super luxurious to look at and in size. The hallway storage closet was bigger than the tiny cabin she'd been assigned on the pleasure cruiser that had flown her away from Earth. It had consisted of a twin bunk and overhead storage, and she had to share a bathroom with nine other solo passengers.

Magna finished wiping down the counters and faced her. "The kitchen is sanitized. What else may I do for you, Mistress Anna?"

"Please just call me Anna."

The android blinked. "New user information updated. Thank you, Anna. Is there anything I can do for you? Would you like a drink? A snack? A fully prepared meal?"

"No, thank you."

"Have a good evening, Anna. Call out my name if you need me." The android spun around on her wheeled feet and rolled to a panel on the wall. It auto-opened, and the android disappeared inside. The panel closed after it.

Anna wandered around the living space. It was roomy. She finally took a seat on the comfortable couch, making sure she faced the entry door. Fig had said he wouldn't be gone long, but it had been at least half an hour since they'd parted. She missed him already.

"I'm being ridiculous. He had things to do," she muttered aloud.

The door across the room opened minutes later, and Fig walked in. Anna got to her feet, resisting the urge to run into his arms. "Did you get ahold of Free?"

He smiled as he quickly closed the distance between them. "Yes." His gaze left hers as he paused a few feet away from her, looking around. "Are we alone?"

"I sent Gemma home about ten minutes ago. I told her I wanted a little time to myself."

Fig inched closer, gently clasping her hips with his hands. Concern wiped away his happy expression. "Are you okay? What's wrong?"

"Nothing. I'm great."

"Are you certain? Did Gemma say or do anything that upset you?"

"No. I really like her." Anna reached up and rested her hands on his chest. "She's starting to believe I'm honestly happy to be a clone. It wasn't as easy for her to come to terms with that."

"Are you sure that she didn't upset you? I expected Gemma to still be here while I was gone to keep you company." His gaze searched hers. "We don't keep secrets. You can tell me anything. I'm your husband."

That had her smiling. "You most definitely are. I'm really great. I promise. Gemma is wonderful and kind. It's that it was just the two of us on your shuttle, then all those people at dinner, and I wanted some quiet time to process everything. You know?"

"You felt overstimulated by being around so many people. I understand. Do you want me to give you more time alone?"

"No. I never need space from you."

He pulled her flush against him. "How do you like home base so far? I'll give you a tour tomorrow. Our first stop will be to visit one of the clothing manufacturing bots. You can pick out any style of clothing they have available."

"Gemma told me about them and offered to lend me a nightgown until you take me there to pick out a wardrobe tomorrow. I told her I'd just wait until then since we sleep naked."

His hands tightened their hold on her hips, and Fig leaned down a little, putting their faces close together. "I love sleeping skin-to-skin with you while holding you in my arms."

"We should do that now and test out the bed. You know, to make sure it's comfortable." Anna winked. "Not the sleep part but the skin-to-skin."

"I love you and your ideas."

Anna slid her hands up his chest to grip the top of his shoulders. "Take me to bed, handsome."

"My pleasure." Fig lifted her right off her feet.

Anna chuckled as she wound her arms around his neck, and he carried her to their new bedroom. The lights automatically came on as they entered it. Fig was strong and made her feel dainty as he gently placed her at the end of the bed. He released her, stepped back, and started to strip.

"I'm never going to get tired of watching you," Anna admitted, removing her own clothing.

"I'm grateful that you find me appealing."

"It's so much more than that. I find you mega sexy. You're perfect, Fig. I will say that no leaf is ever going to hide that." She pointed at his hard-on.

He grinned. "I feel the same way about you. You're perfect and mega sexy."

Anna slid off the bed and reached for Fig. She loved touching his warm, firm skin. Every muscle sculpted on his fit body looked like art to her. He was a masterpiece of flesh, blood, and a wonderful heart. She highly doubted that DJD Clone Corp would ever understand the true beauty they'd created in their factories. Fig was better than a human. She would know since she used to be one.

She reached up, caressing his face. "Kiss me."

Fig leaned into Anna, wrapping one arm around her waist, his other hand cupping the side of her face. "My pleasure."

Then his lips were on hers. All thought left Anna's head as he deepened the kiss. He lifted her off her feet and stepped forward until they both came down on the bed. She wrapped her legs around his waist and used her fingernails to rake them over his skin. Fig groaned against her tongue.

It didn't take long for her body to be primed and ready for Fig. She rubbed against him, seeking more. He adjusted his hips. She was so wet that he slid home easily, filling her. She loved the feel of his thick, hard cock.

He moved slowly at first, taking her even deeper. Every thrust of his hips brought her closer to climax. They fit together in a way that made it seem as if they'd been made for each other. The way he moved had him rub against her clit as he fucked her. She tore her mouth from his, moaning his name.

He nuzzled her throat until she turned her head to give him access. He lightly bit the tender skin near her ear right as one of his hands squeezed her breast. The pinch of her nipple did it. Sheer ecstasy rippled through her. Her muscles squeezed around him tighter, and she felt him come with her.

He rolled as they clung to each other, making sure he didn't crush her with his weight. Anna ended up on top, sprawled and panting to catch her breath as they started to recover.

"You are so good at this."

He chuckled. "So are you."

"We should sleep in late instead of getting me some new clothes tomorrow. The idea of staying in bed with you all day sounds perfect. Can the Magna deliver us food in here?"

He tensed under her.

Anna lifted her head, peering into his eyes. "It was just a suggestion. What's wrong?"

"I need to provide backup for Free when he meets with that shuttle. Blade is taking his vessel there, too, so the three of us can easily handle a fight if it turns out to be a trap. I won't be gone for more than a few days. Gemma will help you use the clothing bots and keep you company. I need to leave first thing in the morning with Blade."

She blinked a few times, letting what he'd said sink in. "No."

"They need me."

"Of course they do. I meant no, you're not leaving me here. I'm going with you."

"It's safer for you to remain here."

Her temper flared. "We're married. Till death do us part, Fig. I only want life if you're in it. That means I go with you."

"I'm certain we won't be outnumbered since we'll arrive in three shuttles. Even if we are, Blade has the *Morgan*. It's a top-of-the-line Varlius class shuttle with heavy defensive weapons. It's the best model Earth makes. I'd prefer for you to stay here where I know you'll be safe."

Anna sat up, straddling him. They were still intimately connected. "I prefer to go with you." She crossed her arms over her chest but then smiled. "This is our first fight."

"You find that amusing?" He didn't look happy at all.

"Yes." She started to slowly roll her hips. "We are making up and fighting at the same time. Here's something you will learn about me, handsome. I'm stubborn when my mind is made up. I'm going to ride you until you see it my way."

He gripped her hips, and his eyes narrowed as his cock hardened more inside her. "You're distracting me. That's not fair."

"Love isn't fair. Neither is abandoning me while we're still on our honeymoon. I'm going with you. Let me tell you about marriage vows." She slowly moved up and down, biting back a moan because she loved having him inside her. "There's this part about being there for each other in sickness and in health. In our case, it's going to include sharing dangerous moments together."

He started to thrust up under her, driving into her deep. Anna lost her train of thought as she moved faster. Fig felt too good. He released her hip with one hand and used his thumb to rub up against her clit.

"Yes!"

"I can play unfairly, too, my love. I want you safe."

They didn't speak again until they both came for a second time. Anna collapsed on his chest, nuzzling her face against his. Long minutes passed as they both recovered.

Anna finally spoke. "I'm going with you. I'm hoping everything will be fine, but I want to be at your side if you face danger. We live or die together, handsome."

He held her in his arms just a little tighter. "I can't stand the thought of losing you. I wouldn't want to live without you."

"Exactly. Right back at you. You go, I go. We're joined at the hip."

He sighed.

"For better or worse. Danger or not. We stay together."

"We stay together. This better not be a trap. I've never wanted to kill humans, but I swear I will wipe them all out if they set a trap for us. No one is taking you from me, Anna."

"I'd kill for you too. Promise you won't sneak out and leave me. Your word."

He gave her a squeeze. "I give you my word. I'm not happy about it, but we stay together."

She felt relief. "I love you."

"I obviously love you too, or I'd never agree to this. I feel like I'm already failing as a husband."

That had her jerk her head up and meet his gaze. "You're not. Great marriages are made of partnerships, Fig. It's being there in the good times and the bad. The rougher the situation, the tighter we need to stick together."

"I understand."

"Good. I want to protect you, too. We can't watch each other's backs if we're apart."

"You win, Anna. I am not happy, but I have sworn to take you with me."

She laid her head back down on his chest, listening to his steady heartbeat. "How early are we leaving?"

He hesitated. "We want to get there before Free does. It's going to be close. He wasn't thinking clearly when we gave him the news about Marisol. I'm thinking he'll stress his engines to get to her as fast as possible."

"He loves her."

"Yes. Even after she broke his heart."

"Love isn't always painless or easy to obtain. It took me eighty-five years to find you. I'm hoping she realized what she lost and now wants to get back together with him. Then again, I'm a bit of a romantic."

"Computer, decrease the lights to ten percent," Fig ordered.

The overhead lights dimmed.

"We should get some sleep. Are you cold?"

Anna shook her head. "The room is perfect, and I don't want to move. I love being right here."

"I make a good mattress."

She yawned. "Yes, you do. I'm tired. It's been an eventful day. How about we nap for a few hours and then go back to your shuttle? We need to beat Free back to that shuttle."

"Is there any way I can change your mind and have you stay here while I go?"

She caressed his skin, loving the feel of him as she started to doze off. "Not a chance in hell, handsome."

Fig knew the moment Anna drifted to sleep. Her breathing slowed, and she stopped moving her hand. He did love it when she petted him. The promise he'd made had been sincere, but he didn't have to like it. Anna made some good points, but he hated the idea of taking her into danger.

He couldn't break his promise, though. She might never forgive him if he left her behind. She said marriage was a partnership, and he agreed. That meant they should do things together.

He stroked the soft skin of her back near her spine. *Even dangerous things. It might just be the cost of having her in my life. Marisol wouldn't have been able to find us if I hadn't saved Anna from permanent death.*

He forced all thought from his head, knowing that he needed to get some sleep. There would be little of it in the following days until he could safely bring his Anna back home.

"Computer," he softly called out. "Set an alarm to wake us in four hours."

There was a soft chime to let him know it had taken his command. He decided to leave the lights on low in case Anna woke from needing to use the bathroom. It would take her time to learn about their new home and the layout.

He just hoped they would have the long future together he couldn't stop thinking about.

Chapter Ten

Anna sat in the secondary seat on Fig's shuttle. She knew it had been difficult for him to allow her to stay at his side when they might face flying into a trap. It's why she kept telling him how much she appreciated that he hadn't broken his word.

Fig looked much more worried than she felt. She turned her head, seeing the huge shuttle flying next to them. Blade kept pace with them in the much larger vessel. They weren't out there alone to face whatever waited. She felt confident they'd be okay. There was no other option. She'd finally found happiness. Nothing was going to take that away from her.

The comms dinged. Fig immediately answered.

"We should be seeing something on our long-range sensors soon," Blade stated. "Should we risk attempting to raise Free?"

Fig seemed to consider it. "No. The only reason I feel confident speaking with you is because we're transmitting extremely weak signals that no one else will be able to pick up. I don't want to give away our location or the fact that two of us are approaching the destination."

"Agreed. They'll pick us up on their sensors soon as well, but with us traveling so closely together, they should have mistaken us for one vessel instead of two. They won't realize the truth until we're in visual range."

"That was a good plan."

Blade chuckled. "I have my moments. Being forced to work with pirates taught me some tricks."

Fig glanced at Anna before he winked. "Was your Hailey upset that you left her at home?"

"A little," Blade admitted. "Her parents were on my side, though. They are very protective of her. Both promised to keep her busy so she doesn't worry too much."

Anna shot him a smile, knowing he was teasing her by asking that question. He'd gotten a little grief from Big when he'd realized Anna was tagging along. Fig had taken it good-natured, though, explaining he would never tell his wife what to do.

The past few days traveling had seemed to make him feel better about bringing her along. They'd made love more often at first, depending on Blade to keep an eye out for danger. Fig had even felt safe enough to give him remote control of the autopilot while they'd spent time in the cabin. The bed was more comfortable than the pilot's seat for frisky times.

"I have something." Blade's voice deepened. "Shit. Are you seeing this?"

Fig leaned forward, his hands flying over the controls. Anna wasn't sure what he was reading on the console, but whatever it was, his jaw clenched, and his body got ramrod stiff.

"What is it?" She couldn't contain her curiosity for more than a few seconds.

"Long-range sensors are picking up three shuttles. Not one or two."

"What does that mean?" Anna leaned forward in her seat, trying to glimpse what was holding Fig's full attention.

He glanced at her and pointed to the red dots showing on the console in front of him. "This is nearest to my retreat. I believe it's the shuttle we encountered." He moved his hand over to two other red dots. "These seem to be heading toward the first one."

"A fourth just showed, but I believe that one must be Free," Blade cut in. "It's coming from the direction of the Balarian system."

"So it must be a trap." Fig ground out a muttered curse.

"No. I think it's two pirate teams going after the shuttle we planned to meet with." Blade cleared his throat. "Those two advancing shuttles aren't flying closely together, but they are coming from the direction of a known hub."

"What's a hub?" Anna had never heard of that term before. Everything out in outer space was different from Earth.

"That's what pirates call a base they control." Blade hesitated. "You said that other shuttle repeatedly attempted to contact you, correct?"

"Yes. Every six hours, at least while we were hidden inside my retreat. Why?" Fig scowled. "What does that matter?"

"Pirates have communication buoys they drop through space to pick up distress signals or other communications. It's possible they might have realized a ship was out here and mistaken the repeated calls to you for a damaged vessel seeking help. That would make it an easy target for them to attack and raid from."

"That was a week ago. Wouldn't they have come after it before now?"

"No, Fig. Some of those monitoring buoys conserve power by only sending signals every ten days or so. It's possible the pirate hub was only recently made aware of communication activity in this sector."

"That's not good."

Anna silently agreed with Fig.

"It could be much worse. Two pirate teams are better than five or six. No more of them are showing up on my sensors. I doubt they wanted to waste the manpower to go after one or two vessels that they may believe are still here." Blade paused. "You responded to the hails at some point, correct?"

"Yes," Fig admitted. "We kept it short and coded."

"It won't matter. One of those buoys would have registered both shuttles if you transmitted anything to each other unless you were as close as we are now and sending extremely weak signals. It looks like we will have a battle to fight unless they decide three on two aren't good odds."

"Three? There's four ships, including us, who aren't pirates."

Fig met Anna's gaze. "We're currently registering on sensors as one shuttle instead of two. There's no way anyone on the shuttle we spoke to before is working with pirates. No one but Blade can hear us, but it's too risky now that they are so close to say any names. Don't."

She nodded.

"You are correct, Anna. It's four on two because three of us are certainly working together, and that shuttle we came to meet with can't risk being captured," Blade softly explained. "For obvious reasons. Let's go silent and pick up our speed. I see that Free has done that. He must have come to the same conclusion: the two unexpected shuttles belong to pirates."

Fig cut comms. "There's no way that Marisol could trust any pirate, no matter how many credits she offered to bribe them with to leave her alone. They would capture her, keep her a prisoner at one of their hubs, and attempt to keep blackmailing her grandfather for as long as he lived. By then, they'd have tried to break her spirit until they could strip her of her wealth and ownership of Clone World."

"That's terrible."

"You're forgetting what I told you about Rico Florigo. Marisol knows how heartless her grandfather can be. He'd allow her to die before he let pirates siphon money from him. She'll fight them right alongside us to keep from being captured. Four shuttles against two pirate ones."

"Are we sure they are pirates?"

"Blade knows them well and the locations of their hubs. I can tell you that the direction they are coming from isn't a used travel path. I chose this area because the only traffic coming near this system is transports to and from Clone World. Pirates aren't interested in our plasma, medical supplies geared for our kind, or the merchandise sold to tourists. Not unless they really need items with the Clone World's logo printed on them."

"What about food?"

"Those transports are heavily guarded. Pirates aren't stupid enough to attack them."

"I see." Anna was learning.

The console dinged with an incoming transmission. Fig's features harshened. "What is she doing?"

"Who? Marisol?"

He nodded at Anna. "That's coming from her shuttle."

There was a softer ding. Fig answered it, speaking directly to Blade. "I don't think she's aware those are pirates."

"That was my thought as well. How do you want to handle this? She's not moving away from them. The pirates will reach her before we get there. Is it possible that she believes they are with us?"

"Yes," Fig decided. "I'm alerting her."

"Be careful of your words," Blade warned.

"Obviously." Fig answered the transmission from Marisol's shuttle, speaking first. "Alpha, Roger form, line six. The two incomings are slightly spaced apart. Do you understand?"

There was a long pause. "Are you sure?" The woman sounded scared.

"Affirmative. Red, nine, seven, zero, bar, ten." Fig paused. "Seven, seven, seven on the other inbound."

"Understood," Marisol said in a shaky voice. "Are you saying nine, six, zero?"

"Nine, six, zero," Fig repeated back. "Confirmed."

The communications ended. Anna got up from her seat, walking to stand beside Fig. "What was the alpha stuff about?"

"A.R form, line six is losses due to thief. That's the only way I could warn her without directly saying those are pirates. The other code is for the defense budget. I'm hoping she understands that she'll need to fight until we get there. The three sevens are what we use to await input from one of us. I'm hoping she figures out that I want her to know that's another one of us coming to her."

"And the nine, six, zero?"

"It's what is used when that date is urgently needed. I confirmed that we're going to reach her as quickly as possible."

"Why can't you just tell her it's pirates and to attack them?"

"It might draw more pirates to this location if they believe those two teams are about to be attacked. With the codes we used, it will just confuse them. I'm also worried the law authorities might also be able to pick up information when those buoys transmit. Saying pirate activity is happening will bring them here. That is the last thing we need."

"You don't think anyone else could break the codes you're using?"

"They are all from Clone World's finance department. Marisol ran it. Very few humans who work there bother to learn even a portion of them, and they sure don't allow clones off-world."

She stared at the viewscreen. "How long until we reach that other shuttle?"

"A few hours. It's going to be okay. I'd get us out of here if I didn't believe we could take two pirate ships. Your life is my priority."

Anna leaned in and wrapped her around his broad shoulders, giving him a hug. "I'm not worried, handsome. Four against two are great odds."

"I don't even think we're going to have to fight." He pointed. "Free has increased his speed. He'll get there before we do, and he's very motivated to save her."

"That's love."

Fig turned his face, their gazes locking. "Yes, it is. A male will do anything for his female. I'm so grateful we found each other."

"Me too. I love you, handsome."

"I love you. We'll spend days in bed like you wanted as soon as we get back home."

"Yes, we will." Anna smiled, certain that they would be doing that very soon.

Free

By:

Laurann Dohner

Prologue

Three Years Ago

Marisol entered the finance department and plastered a smile on her lips. "Hi, Manny."

The guard nodded and buzzed her through the second door. She kept a false façade of happiness on her face as she passed men and women sitting at desks in an open area of the financial department. She stopped at a secretary's desk. The woman looked up.

"Please inform Freak I'm here and ready to go over last week's profit and loss reports."

"Of course, Ms. Florigo."

She entered the private meeting room and laid down her briefcase on the long table. The door behind her opened less than a minute later. She took a deep breath. "Thank you for not keeping me waiting."

She turned, staring into a pair of beautiful gray-blue eyes on a very handsome face. Having tan skin and blond hair amplified the pale color of his irises. He stood tall at six-foot-two. The form-fitting uniform he wore displayed a fit body. He closed the door and laid down his data device on the table.

"It's been the longest two days."

Marisol ran into his arms, and he held her when she pressed up tight against him. "I missed you, Free." She refused to call him what the others had labeled him with when they were alone. He had a highly intelligent mind and could calculate numbers faster than a computer. It didn't make him some kind of freak. He was a genius.

"I missed you too."

She loved being held by Free and hated that they could only steal brief moments alone. "The captain believes the bullshit story about one of the employees hating killing clones and is hiding a bunch of them on the planet to explain why that much plasma from Earth is needed. He seemed sympathetic, but mostly, he was in it for the money. He's purchased it and added six crates to his shipment."

Free appeared nervous. "Is he trustworthy?"

"He better be for what he's asking me to pay him. Greed can be an extreme motivational tool."

"Is there any way he can figure out that you're the one he's been communicating with?"

"I've covered my tracks too well. He believes I'm a much older man who is in charge of retraining clones for new jobs. I said the program was doomed to fail, so that's why I'm protecting them from being permanently decommissioned."

"There is no such program on Clone World."

She nodded. "I know that. You know that. He doesn't. I thought about saying I was a doctor to account for why I'd go to such lengths to save lives, but once you steal the shuttle, he'll be interrogated after he's rescued. I didn't want all the medical staff dragged into the investigation if they get him to tell the truth. I doubt they will, but just in case, I don't want someone possibly taking the fall for what I've done."

Free lifted his hand and brushed his fingers over her cheek. "You're so thoughtful, Marisol." His expression grew remorseful. "I hate putting you at risk. No matter what you say or how much you assure me, I'm worried. No plan is foolproof."

She could tell that he was concerned. "It will be fine. This captain transports illegal high-end goods for my gramps, so his shuttle is equipped to evade weapons fire in case someone becomes suspicious. His name is Captain Edward Rule."

"I'll remember."

"Just stick with the plan. He believes the six of you are working for me to retrieve my plasma shipments right before he takes off. He's expecting you to be on and off his shuttle in under five minutes total to unload the hidden cargo. That won't leave you much time to take control and fool flight control into thinking it's him taking off on time."

"The B Clones already have worked out those details since this captain is a regular visitor to Clone World because of your grandfather's illegal deliveries. They will synthesize his voice and speech patterns. No one will realize they are piloting the shuttle instead when we leave."

Marisol nodded.

"We'll eject him inside the emergency pod when we're safely in orbit and out of weapons range." His light blue eyes held her gaze. "We won't harm him."

"I know. Your life is the priority, though. Don't forget that. If it comes down to one of you or him…"

Free scowled.

"I mean it. While I don't want Captain Rule dead unless it's absolutely necessary, he's a smuggler. He might not deal in living beings since my gramps doesn't use him to transport unblanked clones, but he does bring in drugs and other highly illegal substances that my gramps keeps on hand to make some of his wealthier clients happy. He's not a good guy."

"I understand." His features turned grim. "We'll do what we must to gain our freedom so that you and I can have the future we want."

That was her ultimate dream. One day soon, they would be together without constant fear of someone catching up on how they felt about each other. Free would be killed if anyone even suspected that she cared so deeply for him. "I've transferred more money into our secret account. You might need access to it while we're apart in case an emergency comes up. Bribery works on most humans. Don't forget that."

He frowned. "I hate you taking extra risks. What if you get caught for transferring those stolen funds before you're able to escape? Your grandfather is ruthless."

"Let me worry about my gramps. We'll be together full-time soon enough." She wanted to kiss him. "That's all that matters."

"I love you, Marisol. I wish you would leave with us now."

"My gramps is going to be furious when he discovers some of you escaped, but he won't send teams after you because he'll figure you won't survive for long. That captain isn't going to admit to having plasma onboard. He'll lie and say it was something else. Gramps is his best client, and that would end their business dealings. Gramps would use every resource available to track us down if he suspects I'm with you just out of spite."

"I still don't understand that."

"Gramps has a temper when it comes to anyone betraying his trust. He'll feel super motivated to hunt me down because his expectations of me are extremely unrealistic because I'm his granddaughter, regardless of how terrible he can be."

"He expects absolute loyalty," Free guessed.

"Exactly. We need to stick with the plan. You go first, and then I'll disappear at the travel conference when we meet up there in two months. He'll blame one of the other entertainment planet representatives for my disappearance. It's a cutthroat competition to get major corporations to sign contracts. It wouldn't be the first time someone was assassinated at one of those events and their body never found."

"Why would your grandfather put you in that kind of danger by sending you there?"

"Huge sums of revenue are involved when corporations agree to hold all their retreats here if I get them to sign. You know money always comes first with him."

"What if your grandfather decides to send someone else to Barlish?"

"He won't. I've landed six huge contracts in the past year alone. I'm the best. Greed is always his main motivation in the business decisions he makes."

"I'm going to miss you very much. Two months will seem like forever."

Tears filled her eyes, but she blinked them back. "I love you too. I can't wait to sleep in your ar—"

Voices sounded from outside the office, and they jerked apart. Marisol took a seat on the other side of the table and dragged her briefcase over, opening it. Free dropped into the chair next to where he'd stood and tapped the pad of his data device.

The door opened, and Manny leaned in. He was the guard assigned to her most of the time while she was working. "Is everything okay, Ms. Florigo?"

"Of course. Why wouldn't it be?"

He shot a glare at Free. "You know the rules. The door is supposed to be kept open."

It angered her. "That's the stupidest policy. I don't want the entire office overhearing private financial records being discussed."

"It's for your safety."

"Do you feel like lunging across the conference table to strangle me, Freak?"

"Not today, Ms. Florigo."

Marisol chuckled, but the guard actually reached for his weapon.

"That was a joke, Manny. Lighten up." She launched to her feet. "Freak wouldn't hurt me."

"I don't trust those things. Neither does your grandfather. He'd prefer replacing the males with the female versions. They tend to cause less trouble."

"Freak is the best clone for this position. Are you aware of why he got dubbed his name? The last female clone couldn't instantly memorize everything she had read. He can, and the account manager dubbed him a freak for being able to calculate sums that large without a calculator."

"Females are less dangerous. That's a fact. I think your grandfather should stop having male clones made for office work."

"I'll be sure to tell him you said that, Manny."

The guard paled. "It's not meant as an insult to your grandfather or his decision-making skills. It's just that males tend to be more aggressive than the females. I'm thinking of your safety, Ms. Florigo."

"I'm fine, Manny. We're just going over food sales. The small vendors had a drop, but our restaurants are doing fabulously. The new warmer weather menus seem to be a hit. The exciting topic of clothing is coming up next. T-shirts versus hats is always a real report page-turner." She collapsed back into her seat. "Do you want to listen in? Otherwise, you're disturbing my meeting, and I have a lot to do today."

Manny spun around and left. The door remained wide open in his wake.

They stared at each other, and Free grinned. "The small food vendors did better than our restaurants. We had four pleasure cruisers that recently docked. Fine dining is something they get onboard those massive vessels. My guess is they craved the snack options."

"As if Manny will remember any of what I said and discuss it with someone else. He's a moron."

"True."

Marisol lowered her voice to a whisper. "In two months, no one will be watching us anymore."

He stared into her eyes. "I can't wait."

"Me either." She smiled, aching to round the table and get close to him again. Of course, she couldn't. Soon, though, their lives would change. Free would be free. They wouldn't have to hide their relationship. There would be no more guards or stupid rules to follow.

No one could judge them for how they felt about each other.

"We just have to wait for a little bit," he reminded her, seeming to know how difficult waiting would be for her. "The time will pass quickly. At least that's what I tell myself."

"You're right. I just want a future with you so badly that I sometimes feel very impatient to start our future together."

"I feel the same." His beautiful gaze held hers. "I'll be thinking about you every minute. It's what I already do."

She blinked back tears. "I love you."

"I love you too."

Chapter One

The Present

Marisol read over the data one more time. She hadn't checked that account in nearly a month. At first, she'd done it in desperation, hoping to see a withdrawal or charge on the account. It would prove that the man she loved was still alive. Her hope had faded rapidly after the first year. That's when he would have run out of clone plasma and needed to purchase more. Then, it had just become a habit. Nothing had changed until that day. Someone had finally accessed it.

It hurt so deeply that she hadn't been able to touch her dinner. The meal sat cooling on her dining room table from where the housing staff clones had left it for her over an hour before. A small group of them brought her meals, cleaned her home while she was at work, and did her laundry.

No one else was aware of the discrepancy she'd found earlier that day. The missing large sum had been funded through a hidden marketing account, the same one she'd used to pay for the man she loved to escape Clone World.

Only her, Free, and Figures knew how to access that money to prevent it from being flagged. Those funds officially didn't even exist. She certainly hadn't used it. That only left two other suspects. At least one of them was still alive. It was the only explanation.

It had taken time, but she'd traced what had been purchased. Her grandfather bought illegal unblanked clones from time to time. Those were clones created with memories from their original human-sourced bodies.

She pretended not to know about the ones in her grandfather's private collection. It turned her stomach, imagining why he'd want off-the-books female clones created, but there wasn't anything she could do about it. It horrified her that he probably used them as sex slaves. He sure couldn't parade them in public or introduce them to the guests.

Her gramps bribed officials at JDJ Clone Corp on Earth to do highly illegal things. He probably also paid off the law authorities, so they didn't check those shipments coming from the clone factories on Earth. They'd just look the other way if she managed to slip intel to them about his activities or warn him that he had someone leaking information.

Not that she'd do that. Her gramps would have no problem killing the illegally made clones to destroy the evidence if anyone bothered to investigate. It wasn't like he cared about them or even saw them as living, breathing people with feelings. They were products created to do jobs and nothing more. He didn't even consider it murder when one was executed for failing to perform the way they were intended.

It was prohibited and punishable by severe prison time to have any clones made with memories still intact from the original source materials. Those would have been living humans. It was considered unnaturally cruel. Those clones would awaken believing they were the same people they'd once been, unaware that they'd died. The shock alone of learning they were now property instead of free individuals would be enough to make their sanity snap.

There were other factors, too. In some cases, the time lapses between their deaths and when they were awoken as a clone could be drastic. Everyone and everything they knew would be long gone in the past. Rumor had it that DJD Clone Corp had been collecting DNA and the brains of certain high-profile individuals for a century.

That would have been anyone the company felt might be historically relevant in the future. Politicians. Celebrities. Entertainers. She knew of one horror novel author her grandfather had purchased a clone copy of with memories. That wasn't for sex, at least. Her grandfather wasn't attracted to men. She suspected he was forcing the poor soul into writing more books for his private reading or for some twisted financial gain in the future.

"He's a monster," Marisol whispered.

Clone World would be shut down if it ever came to light what the owner of the planet had unblanked ones created. The authorities would terminate all the clones her gramps had bought. Every. Single. One. No matter how much she hated what kind of lives those dozen or so illegal clones lived, it was better than watching all of them be slaughtered just because her gramps broke the law. Over eight hundred clones worked on the planet.

Why would Figures or Free pay for an illegal clone to be made? It had been a female. That was all Marisol had been able to figure out on the payment transaction. It wasn't like DJD Clone Corp was going to put an unblanked clone purchase in writing to make the crime easily provable. The billing price let her know the truth. A clone with real memories costs almost three times the normal amount of a programmed one. It also proved that at least one male, if not both, was still alive. She blinked back tears.

Free had never contacted her while she was at Barlish station. She'd grieved him, certain that he'd died. One of his fellow clones would have sent word to the station telling what had happened to him otherwise. At least, that had been her assumption. None of them had sent a message to her hotel room. That's why she'd believed they must have been killed shortly after their escape.

It left only one conclusion to come to after someone had used that account. Free had lied from the beginning, used her, and only pretended to be in love with her. The realization was...painful.

She'd been a fool. One who'd tormented herself with Free's memory and the shattered dreams of a future they should have had together. The pain in her chest became so intense that it hurt to breathe, and she clutched at the front of her shirt.

A small noise alerted her that someone had entered the other room. No one should have been inside her home. Marisol dropped her arm, ran to the weapon she kept hidden behind a picture frame of her deceased parents, and fisted it. The housing staff had no business being in her home after dinner delivery.

She backed up into the corner behind a tall artificial plant and targeted the doorway to the living room. Four people wearing medic uniforms strolled casually through it, each carrying a blue med bag. Two were males, and two were females. All of them had black hair, but their eye colors varied. They didn't see her at first, heading toward her bedroom.

"What in the hell are you doing?"

They froze at the sound of her voice.

Marisol stepped out from behind the tall plant. "Answer me. What are you doing in my home?" She glanced at their uniforms to be sure, the blue strip around their throats and wrists telling her they were, in fact, clones.

The tallest male slowly faced her. "It was a mistake. We're in the wrong home. Our apologies."

She kept her weapon trained on them. "Bullshit. You should have gone after my gramps if you wanted to kill someone. I get it. I do. I *see* you," she said softly. "I know you have feelings and emotions. I didn't buy this damn planet or force you to work here."

All four clones just silently watched her.

"I don't keep you enslaved, and I can't leave either. Do you understand that? My gramps would never allow me to have a life somewhere else. I'm seen as property, too, because I'm family to him. He's an asshole that way. If you ever repeat my words, I will deny saying that, but that's the truth. I'll pretend this never happened, for your sake. Just don't come after me again. Do we have an agreement?"

The tallest male clone nodded. "We didn't wish you harm, Ms. Florigo."

She glanced at the bag he carried, really noticing it for the first time. "That is a clone plasma carrier." She frowned, staring at the tallest medic. "Stop lying. Giving me clone blood will kill me. Why deny it? As I said, I understand your anger, but you're going after the wrong target. I'm not your enemy, damn it. I have sympathy for your kind. Trust me, I do. You should have talked to the clones who deal with me every day, and they would have told you how I treat them as equals."

He sealed his lips.

"Do you understand what I've said? I won't report this because you'll be killed. I don't want that. Just don't come after me again." Marisol needed them to understand.

The second male clone lifted his gaze, holding her stare. "We aren't here to harm you."

"I'm ordering you to stop lying."

"I'm not."

She stared at his face, trying to read him. "Then why are you here?"

"I'm not permitted to say."

That confused Marisol until another thought hit. "Did you think you could kidnap me and force your way off the planet? I hate to break this to you, but it won't work. I guess you don't know Clone World history. Let me clue you in. A group of clones tried that with my parents. They took them hostage and made it all the way to a shuttle. My gramps had it shot down. He sacrificed their lives to stop those clones from getting away." Bitterness rose inside her. "He still stands by his decision that killed his own son and daughter-in-law. He'd order security to attack us despite the odds of me dying to stop you from escaping."

One of the two female clones lifted her head. "We know about that tragedy. It's included in our download information package to prevent it from happening again."

That confused Marisol more. "Then why try this? Security will just blow us out of the sky if we even manage to get inside a shuttle. We'd all die."

"We're not permitted to say."

Marisol frowned at the female. It was something a clone would say if they were under orders. "Who sent you here?"

"We aren't permitted to tell you that," the tallest male clone stated.

"But someone sent you?" Marisol knew that had to be the case if they weren't there for revenge.

The female clone who'd spoken before nodded.

"Was it another clone?" Marisol studied her features, looking for a hint of that being the case.

The female shook her head.

Marisol believed the medic was being honest. There were only about six dozen humans living on the planet. Then again, it could be a tourist. It was possible that her gramps had made someone angry enough to want to hurt him by having her killed. "Who sent you?"

"We aren't permitted to say." The second female clone lowered her head. "May we leave?"

Marisol was growing angry. "You know I could hit the alarm, and you'd be killed, right? You entered my home without permission. That would be seen as an act of aggression on your part. I want answers, damn it. Someone tell me something. *Please*?"

The second female clone stared at Marisol again. Her features softened. "We would be killed regardless if we talk."

The mystery deepened. It left Marisol more alarmed than afraid. *What is going on?* She lowered her weapon. "Please? I didn't hit the alarm. I said I'd forget this ever happened. I just want answers."

The tallest male clone glanced at the other three before looking at her. "You wouldn't like the truth, and you'd betray our trust if we did tell you why we are really here."

Marisol made a decision. She walked up to that clone and offered him her weapon. He gawked, refusing to accept it by taking a step back.

"This is me giving you my trust. Please tell me who wants to kill me and who ordered you to come here. Otherwise, just shoot me. I'd rather see it coming than have to worry about the next time someone launches a sneak attack."

The tallest clone paled a little. The first female stepped closer. Marisol offered the weapon to her.

The female ignored it. "You will tell someone, and they'll know we spoke the truth to you," the clone whispered. "It's forbidden. We're the only four who know."

"I won't," Marisol swore. "Just tell me what is going on."

The female glanced at her clone counterparts. They seemed to study each other. The second female clone walked around them and addressed Marisol.

"I'll tell you, but if you let on that you know the truth, we're all dead."

Marisol faced her. "I give you my word."

"We come in here every three months. We're your classified medical team, Ms. Florigo. You should have eaten your dinner that was drugged to put you to sleep. We give you plasma."

Marisol stared at the female clone, letting her words sink in. Her heart pounded, and she felt lightheaded. The implications shocked her to the core. "Oh shit."

"We're sorry. You weren't supposed to ever learn the truth," the second female clone whispered. "You look ready to faint. May I?"

She didn't wait for permission but came at Marisol, dropping the med bag she held, and carefully wrapped an arm around her waist. Then she led Marisol to a chair at the dining room table and eased her down to sit.

Tears filled Marisol's eyes, but she didn't try to hide them. "When? How?"

The female clone crouched in front of her seat. "Take deep breaths."

She listened, doing exactly that. "What's your name?"

"MC-3."

"M for medic, but what does the C stand for?" Marisol tried to focus on that instead of the horror of what she'd just learned.

"Classified." The female clone paused. "That is the actual title. We four were created to take care of you and were labeled that way. We'd never hurt you, Ms. Florigo. You die, we die. You're our sole purpose."

Marisol understood. Her grandfather had ordered a team of medic clones to be created, and the only job was to take care of her. "Three?"

"Third member of our four-person classified medic team."

She glanced at the other three, then back at MC-3. "When? How? Do you know?"

The female clone took the weapon from her loose fingers and placed it on the floor. "Does it matter? We'll be blamed if anyone finds out that you've realized the truth."

"I just want answers. Please. When did I die? I died, right? I'm a clone. One with memories since I didn't even know I was a clone. That's why you brought plasma. My gramps did this?" Marisol answered her own question before they could. "Of course, he did. He's the only one who could."

The other female clone cleared her throat. "The file we were given says you were on the Barlish station when there was a docking accident."

MC-3 took one of her hands, holding it. "The file states that two of your security officers died that day with you. They were escorting you to a shuttle on your way home when a pilot of another vessel made a fatal mistake. He hadn't completely unfastened the docking clamps. There was a breach in that section of the docking bay, and you were sucked into space."

Marisol tried to remember but couldn't. The last time she'd been to that station had been when Free was supposed to meet her. Only he'd never contacted her. The trip home was a blur of her feeling really sick, but she'd been heartbroken. *Only I never made it home, did I? Marisol died.* Then she'd woken as a clone, not even knowing the truth.

MC-3 released her hand and gently cupped Marisol's face, forcing her to stare into her brown eyes. "You were blown into space. It would have happened fast. The rest of your security team quickly located and retrieved you with a shuttle. They were ordered to put your body into stasis to preserve it and immediately fly to Earth."

Marisol was able to put together what must have happened from there. "So I could be made into an illegal clone. I have memories, although some of them have obviously been altered."

"It's why you're classified."

"I don't have the tattoo or any scarring on my hip from where I would have been grown." Marisol was certain of that.

The clone hesitated. "I would guess that it cost extra to surgically remove all traces of where you were grown inside a clone facility."

Marisol nodded. "You take orders directly from my gramps?"

MC-3 nodded again.

"Does anyone else know?"

The female clone shook her head. "Not that we're aware. We four were created at the same time as you to be your medical team. They sent us on the same transport you arrived in on Clone World. We've taken care of you since the beginning. Our orders come directly from Rico Florigo."

Marisol felt calmer. "Gramps thought I'd go insane if I knew I'd been cloned like the original dozen test clones did."

MC-3 nodded. "His personal collection of illegal clones don't survive beyond a year, at the most. They take their own lives or mentally degrade until they die. You've far exceeded that because you weren't aware that your origin body died."

"It's more than that," the other female clone took a seat on the coffee table, perched on the edge. "We're given access to your grandfather's clones and their medical records to compare your progress. The private collection faced a new, foreign life. The depression and insanity they have experienced wasn't only caused by learning they were clones but because of their new purpose."

"To amuse my gramps by being his sex slaves, right?"

The second female clone gave a sharp nod. "We're alive. So are you. You didn't even know the truth until this evening. Be strong, Ms. Florigo."

"Call me Marisol." It only seemed fitting since they were keeping her alive. "I need plasma, right?"

"Yes." MC-3 nodded. "You do. It's been three months since your last transfusion. We could wait a week before your body begins to degrade if you need a few days. You'll die without the plasma."

Marisol was a clone. It was astounding, horrifying, and her entire world had just been flipped upside down. "Do it now. It's why you came. Let's just get this over with."

"Are you going to confront your grandfather?" MC-3 appeared frightened after asking that question.

"No." Marisol thought she knew the man well, but her gramps had cloned her and kept it hidden. It was possible he would destroy the clone body she currently had and just order another one to be grown from the source material. They'd reprogram her mind to make sure she'd forget. He could say she'd been in a coma or something to explain why she'd lost years of her life, then have her miraculously wake up. "This is our secret."

All four of the clones appeared relieved. "Thank you. This will be more comfortable in your bedroom." MC-3 let her go and stood.

"Wait. I've left Clone World since then. How did I pass customs?" She raised her hands. All humans were chipped and scanned. Only true ones birthed by human parents were imbedded with them.

One of the males answered. "They removed them from your original deceased body and transferred them into your clone body. We weren't aware that was possible until we were given your medical chart."

Marisol let that sink in. Those chips were supposed to only work on actual humans, but her grandfather wasn't one to take no for an answer. "I would like to know your names." Marisol glanced at the other three clones.

The tallest male cleared his throat. "I'm MC-1. That male is MC-2. The other female is MC-4."

Marisol memorized their names and faces. They were her medical team. "How do you hide it from me when you give me plasma?"

"The small needle insertion on your skin is healed by the time you wake in the morning. We drug your food, so you're unaware of this procedure. You've never suspected. We're good at this." MC-1 shrugged.

"Will it hurt?" Marisol got up.

"No. We need plasma every three months, too." That answer came from MC-4.

Marisol led the way into her bedroom, her mind reeling. *I'm a clone. I died. Oh shit.*

Chapter Two

Marisol stared out of Straton Miller's office window four days later. It was a beautiful, sunny day in the botanical garden just outside. Paying guests staying at Clone World strolled the walkway paths below, some even having catered picnics. She had to admit that she felt a little envy that he'd gotten such a great view. Her office didn't have any windows. It had been deemed a security risk to her safety.

She'd hacked into the computer system inside Straton's office. The answers she'd learned helped her add more pieces to the puzzle of what had happened to her at that signing conference. The medical team hadn't been correct. The blame probably lay in the files they'd been given. It came as no surprise that her gramps had even lied to the clones caring for her. The truth didn't exactly come easily for someone so used to being deceitful.

Marisol had found the billing date for the order of her new body. The accident had happened on the space station but not when she'd been about to travel home. She'd died six hours after arriving for the conference.

That meant the initial business meetings and her realizing Free wasn't coming, the pain of it, were real memories. She'd gotten sick the following morning, battling flu-like symptoms. That had been a lie, along with the trip home with her burying herself in paperwork. Those had been implanted memories someone at the clone factory had cooked up. It also explained why she hadn't gotten certain companies to contract with Clone World, which she'd been certain she'd easily land. In her head, she'd let her gramps down by becoming sick. In her heart, she'd blamed her broken heart.

It changed everything. What if Free had tried to contact her after she'd already died? He wouldn't have known she wasn't there to answer. Even if he'd learned about the accident that had taken place, she hadn't been listed as one of the sixteen fatalities.

That didn't come as a surprise. Her grandfather would have covered the truth up if the surviving security team members reacted as fast as the clones had implied. He wouldn't want anyone to know that his only heir was gone. It would leave him open to long-distance relatives attempting to assassinate him to gain his wealth or them coming after him in other ways.

It also hadn't been the docking port that suffered damage on the station. It had been a section of guest quarters on the fourth and fifth decks. Space junk had slammed into it, breaching both areas of those decks. She must have been inside her rental suite to prepare for sleep. Two human security guards from Clone World, ones stationed outside to protect her, were listed as casualties.

The office door opened, and Stranton Miller walked in. He was one of her grandfather's most trusted human employees. He'd worked at Clone World for as long as she could remember. That said a lot since she'd been born there twenty-nine years before.

She spun, grateful that she wasn't still at his desk, and forced a smile. "There you are."

He frowned. "What are you doing in here?"

"I wanted to talk to you about my gramps' upcoming birthday."

"That's two months from now."

"I know. I've been racking my brain trying to think up the perfect gift, and I finally found the answer. I mean, what do you get the man who has everything? Then it hit me. Dolters."

"What is that?" He crossed the room and took a seat, plopping down in his chair.

"They are like domesticated alien monkeys. We have cloned species from Earth here, but not dolters. Gramps would love them. I've done my research, and they are very mild-tempered. They could easily survive and thrive on this planet. Everyone who visits Jabler raves about how adorable they are. We could get Gramps a mated pair. I think he'd love them. Imagine how cute their babies would be down the road. It might open some financial opportunities in the future, too. Maybe they could become mascots, and we could sell toy replicas of them to guests."

Straton leaned back, scowling. "I don't see the draw. We already have a wide variety of animals."

"His dog died last year. Dolters are said to be excellent companion pets, too. We buy him a breeding pair, and any babies they have can be let loose in the animal zoning area once they are old enough. The guests would love to see them. That's why I'm thinking plush toy replica sales would be a smart bet. It's a unique souvenir to remind the guests of their time here on Clone World. Isn't that perfect? I figure you can fly there, personally find the pair that would fit Gramps best, and bring them back so they can adjust to our environment before his birthday."

"I am not flying to Jabler. You know I don't take trips. I'm too busy."

Marisol frowned. "Well, I'm swamped too. It has to be you."

"No. We'll just throw Rico a party like we do every year."

"We will, but Gramps would really love a set of dolters. Do some research, and you'll see what I mean. They are super friendly, can be housebroken to use an actual bathroom because of their intelligence, and are sold pre-trained. They even communicate with sign language. Imagine how much glee he'll get out of showing the pair off to his special guests. You know he loves to own things that few other people have. A mated pair of dolters that can breed are super expensive. Most people can't afford them."

Straton seemed to mull that over. He finally nodded. "You've convinced me. Rico probably would love to receive them as a gift. I'm too busy to go. We'll send one of my assistants."

"Anyone else will let Gramps know what the secret is. You're the only one I can trust. We both know how this works. Someone will believe they can advance their work positions if they do my grandfather any favors. They'd see this as such. It will dull his joy over our gift if the surprise is ruined. Imagine how impressed he'll be that we were able to actually keep something from him. He'll know you were the only person who could accomplish that feat."

That seemed to please him, just like she thought it would. Straton was an egotistical asshole. She also knew he hated traveling. That was putting it mildly. The hard part was getting him on board to buy the dolters and keep it a secret. Then he'd have to find a way to get them secretly purchased and transported to Clone World. He turned on his screen and tapped at it.

Marisol carefully watched his face, but no alarm showed. That had her breathing easier. She'd hacked his computer well enough that he wasn't aware of what she'd done. For the next few minutes, Straton ignored her until he finally looked up.

"It's going to take eight days for a round trip. We have important guests booked for the next four months solid. You know your grandfather depends on me to personally see to their needs. You're going to have to be the one to pick these animals up."

She bit her lip, hoping to look frustrated. It was important to make him think it was his idea that she be the one to take the trip. He'd earned becoming Rico Florigo's righthand man by being ruthless and smart. Long seconds passed as she pretended to give it some thought.

"Alright. This is too important not to do. I don't want Gramps to be disappointed on his birthday. I'll see what I can swing to fly there, but you'll have to cover for me. Gramps will know something is up if I take an unscheduled trip."

His gaze returned to his screen. "You'll have to leave later today. It's early for the yearly audit, but I could send you a formal notification right now to account for why you'd hole up in your office for a week. Can you handle your personal assistant lying for you since you won't really be there?"

"Yes." Marisol hated Nancy. The Earth-born woman went out of her way trying to seduce her gramps, wishing to become his seventh wife. The idiot didn't realize she'd be forced to sign an iron-clad agreement that wouldn't entitle her to a dime. Gramps wouldn't spoil her either by giving her expensive gifts. All his wives got was constant verbal abuse, and him being a serial cheater rubbed in their faces. He didn't even have the decency to pretend to be a faithful husband.

Marisol would feel zero guilt for lying to Nancy and more than likely getting her fired. It was more like doing her a favor in the long run, even if it wasn't deserved. The same went for Straton. If everything went right, Rico Florigo would need targets to take his rage out on.

"I'll need a fast shuttle and a security detail. I'm thinking clone guards."

He frowned.

"Human ones can't be trusted. The entire point of one of us taking this trip is so Gramps gets a surprise." She paused. "I'm thinking about telling Nancy that I'm going on the other side of the planet to stay at Gramps retreat home to work from there. I do that from time to time. That way, she won't even know I've taken a quick off-world trip. As I said, we can't trust anyone."

He scowled at her. "Clones aren't permitted to leave the surface for any reason. Besides, you can't trust them to keep you safe and not try to run away."

"I did my research before I came here. A new batch of security model clones just arrived a few weeks ago. I figured they could guard you on the trip. You know how loyal clones are at first with all that fresh programming inside their heads. They also wouldn't know it's odd to be sent on that kind of job."

"Me?"

"Well, I thought you'd be the one to go. Since you can't and I'm stuck taking this trip, that's changed. I'd feel safer with newly woken clones. It's my ass on the line, right?"

He nodded. "There's one thing you didn't consider. Clones couldn't pass security scans on Jabler. You'd have to leave them on the shuttle while you conduct business. That wouldn't be smart."

"Jabler customs officers only scanned me the last few times I visited there and didn't look twice at my security detail. Everyone recognizes my grandfather's name and is aware of my association. Do you honestly believe they won't be giving me VIP treatment?"

That seemed to appease him. "True. You're the heir to Clone World."

Marisol had to exert effort to resist snorting. Her gramps was never going to allow that to happen. She knew for a fact that he kept a medic with him around the clock, and two sets of cryo units were hidden inside each of his highly secured vaults kept at his main residence and at the retreat home.

After her parents had been killed, he'd felt the need to share his big plan with Marisol. If he died, the already-created clone of himself would be woken from the first cryo unit, so people would believe he still lived if they saw it from a distance. Meanwhile, his deceased body would be put into the second cryo unit and shipped to Earth, and an illegal clone would be made with all his memories intact. He'd exist in a clone body, but no one would be the wiser.

For all she knew, it might have already occurred. Her gramps wouldn't bother to tell her since he was a paranoid bastard. The only thing that made her feel better about him living an extended life was he'd be forced to have the clone aged to advanced years. Otherwise, everyone would guess what he'd done.

One day, she figured he'd fake having a son and then get to take on a younger body when he switched his memories into it. That would afford him the ability to do it. Then again, he may have already set that plan into motion. Rico Florigo always thought ten steps ahead. He'd keep her in the dark for as long as possible, hoping she was foolish enough to work harder to inherit everything he owned. Marisol knew her Gramps too well.

Straton tore her from her thoughts when he spoke. "Anything else?"

"Double my security team." She needed four clones, not two. "One team can escort me while I do business, the other to remain on the shuttle. Then the pairs can split shifts and watch over the statis units the dolters will be transported inside on the trip home." It would also make Straton feel more secure that she'd be fine.

"Any preference for a pilot?" He looked at her, his eyes narrowed. It might have been a hint of suspicion.

"No. What do I care? Just get me a competent one. He or she won't be privy to what the trip is for. That's why I want the statis units watched around the clock. The pilot won't be able to sneak a peek inside to see what they contain. They can't blab if they have no information to share about the contents of the cargo."

"Brilliant." Straton went back to work on his computer by ordering her a shuttle and a security detail.

She hid her smile. "I'll go pack. When do I leave?"

He finished. "Two hours."

"That fast?" She tried to look upset and put out. "Fine. Yeah. It's best if we do this as quickly as possible. What flight pad?"

"Six. Shuttle twelve."

"Thanks. Gramps is going to love our gift. Did you look up dolters?"

"I did. They look like something he'll really get a kick out of. He did love that damn dog." Straton shuddered in his chair. "I don't like pets. They smell."

"That's why I don't own any pets either," she lied. Marisol worked long hours and knew she would neglect them since they deserved time and attention from their owners. "These alien monkeys are going to be the perfect gift. Dolters sing when they are happy. And give back rubs to their owners. We're going to be his two favorite people."

Straton grinned. "This is a great plan, Marisol. Thank you for including me."

"To be honest, I thought you'd be the one going to buy them." She forced a laugh. "I want my gramps to get exactly what he deserves." She winked. "Even if I do have to share the credit for this gift. I'm off to pack. I'll totally get the job done."

Marisol almost made it to the door when Straton called her name. She turned, facing him. Her heart pounded.

"I do expect that audit to be done."

She forced another laugh. It was from relief that time. He'd just played right into her hands. She needed an excuse for taking sealed cargo containers to hide the clone plasma they planned to steal. "Of course. I'll work on the flight and have plenty of time to complete it. That means I need to take my printed files with me since the network won't be secured off-planet. Notify the landing field guard that I'll be having boxes delivered."

That caused him to frown. "That information is confidential."

"Then order them not to open the boxes to view the files. I can seal them to assure privacy and have the clone guards protect the boxes with the stasis units I'll need to transport the dolters."

He seemed to ponder that before nodding. "I'm sending notifications now."

Marisol fled and pulled out her com unit the moment she left the building. "It's a go. All bases covered. Two hours, pad six, shuttle twelve."

"That's not enough time."

"It's going to have to be. This is our one and only opportunity."

"Affirmative," MC-1 whispered.

Marisol ended the call and hurried home. The packing had already been completed. Keeping calm until they lifted off the planet would be tough. She was about to escape Clone World with her MC clone medics. No way would she leave them behind. It would mean their deaths.

Chapter Three

Marisol only glanced at the four clones wearing stolen security guard uniforms as they met at the flight pad. The human pilot stood outside the shuttle parked there. The second he spotted her, he appeared shocked. "Ms. Florigo."

"You are?"

"Don Titon."

"It's nice to meet you. Are we ready to lift off?"

"No one informed me that you were my passenger."

"That's because it's above your pay grade." She gave her best bitchy face glower. "Top secret stuff direct from my grandfather. Let's go."

He hesitated.

"Now," Marisol ordered, her tone firm. "You've got your orders. Follow them, or I'll contact Straton Miller. You do know he is the leading authority right under my grandfather. He will fire you. I'd prefer not to do that if you don't mind. We have a tight schedule to keep. That means not wasting time."

"Of course." The pilot spun and marched inside the shuttle. She followed, her clone 'security team' at her back.

"This isn't a luxury shuttle. My apologies, Ms. Florigo." The pilot turned once again to look at her. "Do you wish for me to request an upgrade?"

"That's not going to happen. Were the boxes and two stasis units that were sent by Mr. Miller loaded?"

"Yes. They are secured inside the cargo hold."

She sighed. "I'm going to share a secret with you and swear you to silence. Are you ready?"

Don Titon's eyes widened. "Of course."

"My gramps is sending me on a secret mission to talk to some of the entertainment on Jabler. Clones are great and all, but we'd like some human talent added here. It's a promotional thing. I'm going in under the radar. That means not showing up in one of our family space yachts."

The pilot nodded along. He seemed to be believing the lies.

"My gramps is depending on us to do this quietly and quickly. The owners of Jabler would be pissed if they realized that we're about to poach some of their top entertainers. We're going to arrive, and by the time they begin to question why I'm there, we'll already be on our way home with two of their top acts hidden onboard. Their security might scan us for life signs, so we need to put them in stasis. No heartbeats to be picked up. Now let's go."

"Yes, Ms. Florigo."

"Silence, Mr. Titon. You don't breathe a word that I'm onboard to anyone. Mr. Miller and my grandfather are the only two people who are aware of my mission. This is going to bring in a lot more tourists. You don't want to be the man who screws that up. My grandfather would *not* be pleased." It was a threat. Rico Florigo had a vicious reputation. Everyone knew it.

"Of course." He hurried to the front of the shuttle.

Once he was gone, Marisol blew out a relieved breath. They just needed to lift off the planet, and then they'd deal with the pilot. She gave her attention to the four clones who stood waiting.

"Take seats and put on your belts. Three of you can fit on the couch." She walked to a lone chair and buckled in.

She noticed the worried expressions of her medic clone team. A lot could go wrong. They had enough plasma stored in those boxes to last the five of them for half a year. Where they'd go or how they'd get more later was something they'd deal with in the future. For now, it was all about escaping.

"Do you—"

"Not now," she snapped at MC-1. Marisol glanced around the passenger area of the cabin. "Ears," she mouthed. It was possible the pilot was listening from the cockpit.

The engines came online, and she breathed easier. When the shuttle lifted off the flight pad, she closed her eyes. Once they reached space, they'd be out of the ground cannon's firing range. She started to pray that they'd make it.

The longest minutes of her life passed until Marisol felt relief when the gravity inside the cabin left. They'd made it into orbit. She opened her eyes right as artificial gravity stabilized. The clones looked a little unsettled over the experience. It was their first time traveling in space. She unbelted from her seat and quickly stood.

"Just like we rehearsed," she muttered, heading toward the cockpit.

MC-4 followed.

The cockpit door stood open, and Marisol stepped in, motioning for the female clone to stay out of sight. "That was a very smooth takeoff."

The pilot twisted in his seat and smiled at her. "That's a compliment coming from you, Ms. Florigo."

Marisol reached her hand back, and MC-4 passed her the syringe. She moved forward, hiding it behind her back. "Wow. I love the view from here. I always wanted to learn how to fly a shuttle."

"Really?" His gaze ran down her body. "I'd love to show you whatever you want."

She hesitated just behind his seat. "What's that red button for on your left? The one by the green one. It looks important."

He leaned forward a little. "That's—"

She struck, jabbing the uncapped needle into his neck, and injected the sedative. He gasped and tried to hit her. MC-4 was suddenly there, grabbing him from behind his seat.

The pilot struggled, attempting to reach something on the front console. Marisol threw her body between him and it, partially landing on his lap as she grabbed his arms. He quickly went limp.

Marisol wiggled off him to stand again, sighing. "How long do you think that will keep him out?"

The female clone stepped forward. "He's larger in size than we estimated. I think anywhere from seven to nine hours at most. For certain, six hours."

"Bring in the males to carry him to the emergency pod. Have them eject him in four hours. The pod will send out an automated distress signal, so by the time he wakes up, someone from Clone World will have hopefully retrieved him already."

"Wouldn't it be safer for us to eject him farther from the planet?"

Marisol knew the clone was right. "I won't risk his life. Once we leave this solar system, the possibility of a pod being picked up by pirates is high. Those thieving bastards are always looking for shuttles that experience mechanical difficulties to target. A pod would be easy pickings for them. I want to make sure this pilot is close enough to Clone World for them to be able to retrieve him as quickly as possible."

It was clear that the clone wanted to argue more.

"I won't kill someone," Marisol firmly stated. "Pirates will demand a ransom if they capture him. My grandfather won't pay to save his life. We'll have a four-hour head start. Straton Miller wouldn't put me on a defenseless shuttle in bad repair. He'd be too terrified of my grandfather's wrath." She took a seat once MC-4 dragged the unconscious pilot from it. "I'm going to shut off the transponder."

"You know how to do that?"

"I've taken a lot of trips, and you'd be surprised by how much pilots will share when they are trying to impress the only known relative of Rico Florigo. I planned to escape once before and learned how to fly shuttles. And how to make it impossible for them to be tracked." She flipped off the autopilot and prepared to reprogram the flight path. "They'll believe we're heading to Jabler, but then I'll change course."

"What is our destination?"

Marisol hesitated. "We're going to intercept a transport heading this way from Earth and watch it. The important thing is that we're off Clone

World. There's enough plasma to last us for half a year. My luggage is filled with energy bars. We won't starve. There's enough water in the tanks on these shuttles to last us for months if we ration it. For right now, we're going to stay on course to Jabler until after jettisoning that escape pod."

"Do you believe your grandfather will think you've been kidnapped?"

"Not when that pilot is questioned by Clone World security. He should remember that I'm the one who stuck him with the needle. I think my gramps will realize I know the truth about being a clone after he learns that not only am I gone, but I took you four with me."

A slight sound had Marisol turn. Two of the clones entered the cramped cockpit to carry the unconscious pilot away. MC-2 and MC-3 were easily able to lift him from the floor. Clones were created to be strong.

"Be very careful with him," Marisol ordered. "Put the pilot in the emergency pod and eject him in four hours," she repeated her original orders, too. "I don't want him hurt in any way."

"It would be better if we didn't do that. You're not expected to be back for eight days, correct?"

She stared up at MC-1, who'd entered the cockpit. He had a grim expression on his face after speaking.

Marisol stood from her seat to face off against the tallest clone. "We're not murderers. I'm also not willing to keep a human hostage onboard. That not only puts us at risk of him trying to fight to regain control of the shuttle, but he'll be a drain on our limited resources. We might all be free now, but I'm still in charge."

She hoped so, at least. There was a small possibility that they could revolt against her. "I could have left you behind, but I didn't. I wouldn't. Because I'm not a murderer. Please tell me that I didn't save you, only to learn that you're capable of killing someone. That pilot's only crime is being desperate enough to work for Clone World. He's just an employee."

The tall clone shook his head. "We don't want to kill. I just believe we'll have a better chance of not being captured if we hang onto the pilot for a few days before releasing him in the emergency pod. There's only one. I checked."

"I know, but if we don't release him soon, we'd have to stop at a station or a colony settlement to drop him off and keep the pod." She lifted her right hand, glancing at her palm. "I have passed identification scanners on stations that say I'm a human when I've taken trips for business, but that doesn't mean we're safe to keep doing that. My gramps could realize at any time that you four are gone and get suspicious before we release the pilot. That means we need to avoid anywhere that alerts can be sent to us. No station stops to drop him off. I knew we'd lose the emergency pod when I started plotting to get us this shuttle."

"We all could die without a pod if the shuttle is damaged."

"I'm aware." Marisol sighed, holding MC-1's gaze. "I warned you that this was risky, and we might die out here in space if we left the surface. That we probably would in time. What matters most to you? Feeling a temporary sense of safety existing on Clone World for as long as you serve a purpose or being free?"

"Freedom," MC-1 answered.

"I have reason to believe some other freed clones are out here in space." Marisol hadn't shared that news with them before. "I have an idea of how to find them. One of them ordered an unblanked clone to be created, and it recently shipped from Earth. It's on the way to Clone World now. We're going to fly toward that transport and hopefully reach it before that illegal clone is taken off it by the escaped ones. There's no way they'd allow that clone to reach Clone World." She paused, studying their faces for a reaction.

MC-1 frowned. "No other clones have ever escaped."

"That's not true." Marisol retook the pilot's seat and checked the long-range sensors. They were heading out of the solar system. "Six of them got away three years ago. I helped them escape. I believed they were all dead, but then that unblanked clone was ordered from the factory on Earth. It was one of those six who did it."

"How do you know that with certainty?" MC-1 crouched next to her.

She turned to meet his shocked gray gaze. "Because whoever ordered that illegal clone used a hidden fund account that was set up just for their escape."

"Hidden?" MC-4 frowned.

"Two of the clones worked in financing with me and helped steal money from my grandfather. Nine plasma cases and one illegal clone were recently charged to that account."

MC-1 appeared confused.

"I didn't place that order. One of the escaped clones did. Each shipment account is notified when an order is fulfilled and given the transport shipping information. It means I can also track the progress of that order."

"That's a lot of plasma for one ordered clone."

Marisol glanced at MC-4. "I'm aware. That amount isn't just for the newly created clone. We've had other transport shipments carrying plasma destroyed since those clones escaped. It was written off as an accident or idiot pirates targeting the wrong ships since that kind of cargo is worthless to humans. It happens. Transport ships carrying what is deemed unprofitable cargo are autopiloted by computers. Now I'm wondering if they were purposely targeted and the plasma cases being shipped to us were stolen by the clone escapees."

"How much plasma could they need?" MC-1 scowled. "How many transports were destroyed?"

"I don't have an actual figure." Marisol shrugged. "My guess now that I know some of the original six clones survived is that they are stockpiling a large supply. That's good news for us when we find them since we need plasma to live, too."

"Is it possible more clones have escaped from Clone World than just those six?"

Marisol shook her head. "No, MC-1. One of my main duties is ordering clones. I always demand explanations if anything needs to be replaced. The staff thinks I do it because I'm a penny pincher, but in actuality, if supervisors abuse clones to the point of terminating them, I refuse to order more to meet the same fate. It makes the humans in charge of clones treat them better. Some increases were expected when we expanded the resort and needed more staff. Those I approved. No clone has been replaced without me fully investigating what happened to the first one."

"You didn't know about us," MC-4 whispered.

"Wrong. I double-checked after learning about you. Officially, you're assigned as part of my gramps backup medical team. The request stated he wanted clones and his human med team in case there was ever an outbreak of one of the flu viruses that originally sprang up on Earth and spread to other resort planets. Clones are immune. With my grandfather's advanced age, it wouldn't trigger any suspicion from me or anyone else when you were ordered. It looked more like a precautionary measure on his part."

"You plan to intercept that cargo? The one carrying the unblanked clone?"

"Yes and no." Marisol hesitated. "The escaped clones will retrieve the one they ordered. I even figured out what section of space where it will most likely happen. I pulled all the information on other plasma shipments that were lost. We should make it there before that transport is targeted."

"Are we going to attack the transport?" MC-4 appeared worried.

"No." Marisol shook her head. "We're going to trail it and watch from a distance. Once the cargo is taken, we'll follow whatever shuttle or transport that has it."

MC-1 scowled. "Will the escaped clones attempt to kill us?"

"No." At least, Marisol hoped not. "We're clones too. Besides, I did help them escape. Wherever they have been living will become our new home. They can accept five more of us."

The two clones left her in the cockpit as she double-checked that no signal was emitting from the shuttle. She stared at the dark space, thinking about Free.

Does he still love me? Did he ever love me at all, or was it a ruse to gain my help so they could escape? Is he even still alive? How will he react when I find him?

Marisol knew it was possible that Free had ordered the illegal clone. That would really piss her off. She'd spent the past three years grieving his loss. He owed her more than to replace her with someone else.

"I'll find out. I have nothing to lose."

Chapter Four

Marisol was bored. Her medical team mostly stayed in the main cabin. The transport from Earth remained on the edge of her sensors, but she hadn't seen any other traffic within range. It was important to keep a far distance, though. She didn't want to spook whoever would want to attack the transport.

They'd ejected the emergency pod with the still unconscious pilot on schedule. Her grandfather was obviously now aware of her escape and that she'd taken her medical team with her. It was terrifying wondering how he'd reacted to first learning the news and what he was plotting.

It was possible that he'd just order another clone of her to be made and shipped to Clone World. Her gramps could always lie to the replacement clone by saying she'd suffered an injury and been in a coma for the past three years. He was that much of a bastard to do something so vile.

That had Marisol thinking grim thoughts. What if the second version of her one day realized what had been done to them? Version two would also want to escape Clone World to find Free. Loving him was a major part of her personality that would definitely get transferred.

"That's why growing unblanked clones is illegal," she muttered.

The only problem with that scenario was her original identity chip from her human body was inside her palm. Clone version two of Marisol Florigo wouldn't have one. It would be impossible for secondary clone her to pass as a human during security checks while visiting other worlds and stations. Then again, maybe her gramps had copied her life chip when he'd shipped her original body to the DJD factory.

He certainly had the money to pay for anything. Marisol was more than aware of just how much wealth Clone World raked in. It was the top earner in vacation destinations. Gramps wouldn't want to lose his best salesperson. That would be her.

"He's totally going to make another me. Damn him."

She regretted not thinking about that possibility sooner. She'd had a lot on her mind, though, like learning she was a clone and that her life had become a lie. She'd reeled from the realization that Free, or at least one of the clones he'd escaped with, was still alive and using the secret account to purchase an illegal clone. And she'd plotted how to get them off Clone World quickly so she could intercept that shipment and have a hope of finding whoever had survived.

"I should have hidden myself a note somewhere in my home in case a version two was made. That way, she'd know one of us was searching for Free already."

"Are you well?"

Marisol startled and turned in her seat to stare at MC-3. The female stepped closer.

"I'm bored but fine."

"You're speaking to yourself."

"That's totally normal for humans. I mutter when I'm thinking unhappy thoughts."

"You're not human."

"Well, in my head, I still am. That counts."

MC-3 seemed to contemplate that. "Do you believe your plan is a failure? That we won't find the other clones?"

"The cargo transport we're intercepting hasn't been attacked yet. I still have faith that it will happen."

"Do you want me to take over flying for a few hours? You slept in that chair all night."

"No. But thank you. I'm sure whoever ordered that illegal clone is going to strike at any time. This is the perfect location. We're past Vista's space station and its authority patrols. I know the escaped clone didn't go to all that trouble to let the transport reach its destination. They had a reason for having that unblanked clone made and will want it."

"Are you worried that you might be wrong?"

"I'd be an idiot not to be," Marisol admitted. "I have faith that I'm right, though."

The clone medic nodded. "Do you believe the authorities are after us?"

"I'm pretty certain my gramps will try to cover this up. He'll hire mercenaries to seek us out rather than go through legal channels. He'd be terrified of Earth finding out what I really am. That would blow back on him big time if someone started an investigation. Gramps can't afford to risk that."

MC-3 didn't look convinced that she was correct.

"He didn't report the escaped clones to the authorities. He just figured they'd die when they needed their next plasma infusions. As you know, these bodies break down and decay without it. That was the beauty of planning their escape. We bought a large supply of plasma for them, separate from what was on the books. None was missing from our stock on Clone World."

MC-3 opened her mouth to ask questions, but Marsol cut her off.

"They'll have audited the amount of missing plasma on Clone World this time to figure out we took enough for a year. Gramps will assume we'll die three months after our supply runs out. Hell, maybe he figures I took off in a fit of rage after learning the truth since I took you four with me and didn't have them check to see if any plasma was missing. I'm hoping that's where his mind goes."

"Why?"

"Why the rage? He made me into a clone without telling me. I'm hoping that he assumes I'll return when my clone body starts to deteriorate rather than die. I am a Florigo. We're survivors. It might delay him from ordering a replacement clone of me to be made. He's probably gleefully contemplating me begging at his feet for him to forgive me when I'm forced to come back. Which won't happen."

"Would he kill you if you're captured and returned? I mean, if you disappoint his expectations?"

Marsol didn't have to think about the answer. "Yes. He's got zero tolerance for betrayal. If you ever thought I was anything like him, I hope you're learning that I'm not. He really is a bastard."

"We thought birthed beings loved their families."

"You said you were programmed with the history of what happened to my parents. Rico Florigo literally blew his own son out of the sky.

Gramps had to have known my dad's body would be too damaged to clone or salvage memories from. But he acted in anger. Gramps always did have a hair-trigger temper. There was no way some clones were going to get the best of him, even if it meant losing his only son. His ego wouldn't allow it."

"I'm sorry."

"It's not your fault. I think opening Clone World and having that much power over the lives of so many people made him utterly heartless. He stopped being a decent person. I'm—"

A beep interrupted her speech, and Marisol spun the chair back, taking the shuttle off autopilot. The transport on the edge of her sensors came to a halt. Marisol reversed the engines to do the same.

"What is it?"

Marisol felt her heart race. "The transport is under attack. The autopilot flying it is sending out a distress hail and requesting authority assistance."

"Will they come?"

"The authority patrol ships are too far out to arrive any time soon, and I doubt they'll care because it is a low-priority transport. Their job is to protect Vista planet residents and everyone living on the station orbiting it. Those kinds of transport aren't supposed to be carrying any life forms. The cargo isn't even for them, so they don't have a reason to get involved."

"Can we go closer to see what's happening?"

"Not without that other ship spotting us on long-range sensors. I don't want to spook them until they rescue that unblanked clone first."

"Understood. I'll inform the others of what is happening." The clone medic fled toward the back.

Marisol felt super excited and nauseatingly nervous at the same time. She was about to make contact with whoever had attacked the transport. Hopefully, it would be Free. If it wasn't, it had to be Figures. Then again, they could have shared the account information from Clone World with the B and R model Clones that had escaped with them.

That last possibility wasn't something Marisol wanted to think about. Whatever she found, whoever had survived, they were the only hope she and her medic team had of finding a safe place to live.

It was possible to stay on the shuttle for long periods of time, but they'd have to dock with a station or land on a planet at some point to restock their food and water. Even to gain mechanical parts if something broke down on the shuttle. Not that any of them had the knowledge to do repairs. Losing life support would be deadly.

It would be too risky to pay someone to do the repairs. Her grandfather would never tell anyone she was a clone, but he would have her arrested on false charges and returned to Clone World.

She wouldn't dare tell the authorities the truth either. They'd immediately kill her. Marisol stared at her hand. The chip implanted there would fool everyone into thinking she was human, but it would also get her caught the first time it was scanned.

The idea of being trapped inside the confined shuttle with the four other clones long-term wasn't exactly safe either. So far, the medics had taken her orders and let her be their leader. That could change in the future. Especially if her plan failed and they were doomed to die with certainty. The other clones would have no reason to want her alive anymore.

"It's going to be okay," she muttered aloud.

Time seemed to crawl by, but after fifteen minutes, she feared that she might not get a lock on the attacking shuttle. It could fly far enough away for her to lose sight of it on long-range sensors.

Marisol gripped the controls and flew toward the transport, still transmitting hails for assistance. She picked both ships up on her sensors within seconds. A privately owned shuttle was currently docked with the transport.

She quickly identified the model of the shuttle, and her hope sank. That wasn't the same type that Free and the others had escaped Clone World on. That meant it might not be them unless they'd somehow acquired a different shuttle.

That seemed very complicated and not like something they'd do. Then again, maybe the original stolen shuttle had been damaged or destroyed. They'd need a replacement if they were still alive. Marisol knew they had the intelligence and skills to steal another.

The other shuttle detached and flew away. The transport it had attacked began to break apart. Marisol ignored it and followed the shuttle. It seemed aware of her presence when it changed course a few times and sped up.

"You're not losing me." She tried to communicate with them, but it was ignored.

"Damn it. Answer me."

All four of the medic clones crowded inside the cockpit. MC-2 leaned over her to study the console readings. "Boost the signal stronger," he ordered as he reached to do just that.

Marisol threw out her hand and slapped his away. "No! We don't want the signal strength strong enough to reach the authority patrols protecting Vista. Then they might fly this way to investigate. That would be bad."

"Why is that other shuttle trying to get away from us? They aren't responding to your hail."

"I see that," Marisol snapped at MC-1. She felt a lot of stress. The pilot of that shuttle was trying to accelerate enough to get off her long-range sensors, changing course, all to lose her. "Let me focus."

"They are clones. Why won't they talk to us?" MC-4 sounded confused.

"They don't know who we are." Marisol took a deep breath and blew it out, attempting to calm her racing heart.

"Fly faster," MC-2 urged.

"I am." Marisol ordered them to be silent.

The next twenty minutes were hellish, and she nearly lost the other shuttle's location a few times, but then it headed toward an asteroid belt. It was marked in the navigational charts as a place to avoid at all costs. The onboard computer system even sent her warnings on her console, recommending she change direction.

"Is the other pilot prepared to die to lose us? Why?"

"I don't think so, and I don't know, MC-3," Marisol responded.

The debris of flying rocks varying in size from a fist to huge buildings was messing with the sensors. There were so many of them that once the other shuttle entered the belt, she lost the ability to track it.

"It's gone. It was destroyed!" MC-1 threw himself into the other cockpit seat and clung to it. "Change course, or we'll be destroyed too!"

Marisol reversed thrusters before they were hit by the flying space rocks. It was like a floating tornado of them in space, blocking their path. She saw a moon on the other side through some gaps in the belt. Her hands flew over the controls, amplifying her view.

"There!" She spotted the intact shuttle flying toward that moon. It was only for a split second, though. "They weren't obliviated. The shuttle made it through!"

MC-4 gripped Marisol's shoulder. "Don't attempt it. We'll die."

"Fuck." She knew the clone was right. Her piloting skills were lacking to prevent their shuttle from being smashed apart. "We'll go around."

"We've lost them. What now?" MC-1 turned his head from the other seat, appearing worried as their gazes met.

Marisol broke eye contact with him and changed course. The asteroid belt was massive, circling around a massive chunk of rock that might be a dead planet. She wasn't an expert. It seemed to her that was the source of gravity that kept the belt in that location. It would take them hours to get around it to reach the moon she'd glimpsed. "We'll find them. I'm not giving up yet. Let's get on the other side of that belt and decide what to do then."

It took just over three hours to reach the moon she'd seen. The four other clones had stayed with her in the cockpit. Three of them were seated on the floor between the two seats.

"Nothing is showing on long-range sensors," MC-1 announced.

"I see that." Marisol wanted to scream in frustration. She'd lost the other shuttle.

"What do we do now?" MC-4's expression and tone of voice expressed her worry. "Do we give up?"

Marisol powered down thrusters, keeping in orbit near the moon.

"Are you giving up?" That came from MC-2. He seemed to have a somber personality. "What do we do now?"

"I'm not giving up. Did you see how that pilot flew fearlessly through the asteroid belt? It's like he has done it often enough to feel confident it won't kill them." Marisol paused, staring at the moon. The scans showed no structures or signals. Nothing lived on it or had been built there.

"What do we do now?" MC-3 asked the question.

"We're going to stay here and wait," Marisol informed them. "At some point, I feel confident that the shuttle will fly this way again. We'll block it before it can lose us through the asteroid belt now that we know what to expect."

MC-1 didn't appear happy as their gazes met. "You don't know if that shuttle will fly this way again."

"It's not like we have anywhere else to be."

Marisol stared at the moon. Huge craters pitted the surface. There were too many to count. It was also possible that the other shuttle had flown into one to hide. For all she knew, that might be where they had set up a home. It was also possible that they occasionally visited an uninhabited planet to find water to refill their tanks and hunt for food.

She started to look up the navigational charts to see if any live planets nearby would fit that bill. There were none. "That's actually good," she muttered.

"What is?"

She looked at the clones, making eye contact. "There's no place for them to resupply water and food when they run low. The closest and only options are Vista or Clone World. No way they are venturing onto heavily protected stations or landing on defensive heavy planets to buy that stuff from humans. That means they must be stealing food and water from other vessels." Marisol leaned back in her seat. "We'll just wait here until that shuttle comes back."

MC-1 drew her attention by scowling. "We're going to die out here doing nothing."

"I'm not doing nothing." She leaned forward again, checking the signal strength of her communication broadcasts. It was best to only send short bursts that wouldn't travel out of that solar system. "I'm going to keep trying to reach out to them at regular intervals."

"Why? They are long gone."

Marisol looked at MC-4 and jerked her head toward the moon taking up most of the front viewscreen. "Maybe not."

"We'd pick up the signature of a shuttle on our sensors if it had landed on the moon."

MC-1 was really starting to irritate Marisol. "Wrong. Check out the readings of how dense that moon is. See those craters? They could hide an entire army of authority shuttles. The dense rock and minerals would fool our sensors into seeing nothing if they were as deep as I suspect. Not that I think any authorities are this far away from where they patrol. It would be a waste of fuel, resources, and manpower."

"That's your plan?"

"Yes, MC-1. That's the plan. We'll keep sending a low burst hail every six hours." She felt a little depressed. "That way, it won't travel far enough to reach the travel path of Clone World visitors or the authority patrols that Vista uses to keep them from being attacked by pirates. Who wants the first shift?"

"I'll take the first one."

It didn't surprise Marisol that MC-1 offered. He was the one she'd have to watch out for if the clones decided to oust her from being in command. She had a feeling that he'd gladly take her place. "I'm going to get some sleep. Wake me immediately if we get a response or something shows up on long-range sensors."

She rose, going to the back of the shuttle. Once she used the bathroom and ate a nutrient bar, she sprawled out on one of the chairs that converted for sleeping. Their escape had gone well, but finding Free and the other five clones he'd left Clone World with wasn't panning out at all.

Marisol slept seven hours and then went back into the cockpit, taking most shifts so she'd be on hand if they got a response. Two days quickly turned into three. Her hope was dying that the other shuttle would return. It was possible that she'd gotten all five of them killed.

The tension between her and the other clones was palpable. MC-1 kept arguing that they should search navigational charts to find a planet on which they might be able to settle. The ones that humans hadn't colonized had been rejected for very good reasons. Either the environment of those planets was too harsh or the wildlife too dangerous. Some had major weather anomalies that made living on the surface impossible. It was impossible to build a city when tornados ripped them apart faster than they could put them up.

MC-1 entered the cockpit and took the other chair. "I have spoken with the others. We've decided it's best if we leave this area."

It was as she feared. They weren't going to listen to her anymore. Marisol met his gaze, her anger rising. They were only away from Clone World because she'd refused to leave them behind to die. *That's the thanks I get.* She debated how to respond, but a beep had her startling.

The sensors were picking up another shuttle. It appeared out of what seemed like nowhere, but it had come from the moon. Specifically, shot out of a deep crater. She immediately sent a hail, her fingers flying across the console as she started the engines, too. There was no way she wouldn't pursue them if they tried to flee.

MC-1 jumped out of the seat and rushed to the back, probably to get the other clones. It was tempting for Marisol to seal off the cockpit to block them. She didn't, though. It would only make the tension between them worse.

Marisol gasped when the other shuttle responded. A male voice filled the cockpit as he spoke. "Why do you keep hailing me?"

Pain sliced through her as she realized that wasn't Free's voice. She'd been so sure it might be him. The disappointment was that great. Marisol swallowed hard before responding, using her words carefully to verify that the male was at least one of the six clones she was looking for.

"I'm one of three. Do you understand?" She let that sink in. Her, Free, and Figures had worked together on Clone World. They'd also come up with the plan that had helped the six clones escape. "I mean no harm. Can we dock together and speak in person?"

The unknown male responded. "Nine, bar, seven, one, dark, quad, ten."

Marisol instantly recognized the exact accounting transaction that had paid the captain of the shuttle the clones had stolen to fly off Clone World. They'd had to memorize them since leaving a trace of that payment would have gotten them caught. "Five, three, zero, bar." That was the rest of it.

"Seven, seven, seven," he ordered before cutting their communications.

"What's wrong? What was that?" MC-1 encroached into her space.

"Get out of my face." Tears filled her eyes. "It's one of them. A clone." Not Free, but one of the six. She'd guess it might be Figures since he'd have also memorized that transaction.

Whoever used that account to play for the unblanked clone had needed to type it in for the funds to transfer when they first reached the shuttle to satisfy the captain. At that point, the money would have been filtered through six accounts in seconds to hide the original source before being deposited into the human's account.

"What was that?" MC-1 backed off a little, but his gray eyes were fixed on her. "Are you certain it is one of them?"

"Yes."

"Then why did he stop talking with you?"

"Seven, seven, seven means to wait for more data. It's what we input while waiting for whatever information we need to complete a transaction." She stared out at the other shuttle in the distance. It wasn't flying any closer, and she didn't want to make them flee by doing that, either. Just seeing it was enough.

"Wait for what data? Hail them again." MC-1 reached for the console.

Marisol batted his hand away. "Stop. Give him time to process. I'm certain he's surprised that it's me. He probably needs to calculate the best way to handle this situation."

"He needs to dock with us and take us to where they are living," MC-1 snapped. "That is the only acceptable outcome."

"We can't force him to do shit," Marisol snapped. "Sit and calm down. Give it a few minutes for him to process what he's just learned. I know F Clones the best since I work with them. They are very logical and cautious."

The other shuttle hailed, and she opened communications.

"I'm not the one you need to speak to. Do you have the capability to wait here for a while?"

The more Marisol heard his voice, the more she became certain that it was Figures speaking. His words implied that Free was still alive. The joy that filled her chest had her barely able to answer. "Yes. Is he alive? Please, tell me." She'd beg to know for certain.

"He's alive."

The tears of relief flowed down her face after hearing confirmation that Free had survived. *He is alive!* "Thank you. Yes, we can wait here."

He paused. "We?"

She chose her words to let him know she wasn't alone. "I have four friends with me that have a lot in common with you." No way could she risk saying clones over communications. Even with being careful of how far she broadcast her signal, at least one shuttle had been hiding inside the moon. It was possible more might be.

Like pirates.

That thought made her sick to her stomach. She'd once overheard Straton and her grandfather snickering over selling some damaged clones to pirates. It had happened after the Solace Celebration a year before. A group of unruly guests had started a bar fight. Three of the female clone serves had suffered bone-deep cuts to their faces and upper bodies from flying glass. It had left them severely scarred. A security male clone had lost a few fingers.

Her gramps and his righthand man had been proud that they'd made a hefty profit. It was standard that a guest had to pay for any property damage they caused on Clone World, including replacing any clones deemed unfit to work anymore with those kinds of physical flaws.

Her gramps held firm beliefs about beauty and perfection. Every clone he bought had to be attractive, unmarred in any way, or they were decommissioned. That was the polite way to say killed. To hear them both saying they'd made a profit had confused her. The guests had paid for replacements. That balanced the books. Then she'd overheard them saying they'd sold the damaged clones. It meant they'd been paid twice.

After digging, she'd learned what the pirates had bought the clones for. Pirates had killed those poor clones while hunting them like animals. Her grandfather had even allowed them to rent a small uninhabited island on their planet to do that horrible deed. Some of his sicker, wealthy friends paid a premium to view and bet on the outcome of which clone had survived the longest.

Pirates finding out they were clones would be terrible. Like those others, they'd use Marisol and her medic team for sport. Their deaths would be drawn out and horrible. Marisol was very careful of every word she spoke.

"Understood," the male finally said after a good minute or two of silence. "Wait here. Don't attempt to follow us."

"We'll wait," she softly agreed, not happy about it. So many things could have changed in the past three years. It was possible that Free wouldn't want to see or talk to her. She couldn't forget that he may have only pretended to be in love with her to gain his freedom.

She was about to find out. That was terrifying.

"You agreed to that?" MC-1 looked furious. "What if they don't return? Hail him back."

"No." Marisol shook her head, glaring at him.

MC-3 suddenly moved, standing between the two seats. She placed both of her hands on MC-1's chest. "Stop. Take deep breaths. We're all stressed, but Marisol knows what she's doing. We're alive and away from Clone World. She did that and was able to make contact with one of the freed clones."

"We no longer have to take orders from humans." MC-1's tone had softened, though. He reached up and placed his hands over hers. It had become clear that the two were a couple. "We know that she still thinks like one of them."

That was proof to Marisol that the medics were talking behind her back. She'd said that to MC-3 after being caught talking to herself. They all seemed to know that she still felt like a human on the inside.

"Fine. We wait and do things her way," MC-1 agreed.

Marisol relaxed in her seat, wondering how long the wait would be until Free or Figures came back.

Chapter Five

"It's been a week," MC-1 pointed out. "That shuttle hasn't returned. No one has come or reached out to us. It's time to find a planet to live on. We'll run out of food and water if we don't."

Marisol was tired of arguing with the tall, opinionated medic. She tried to use logic. "We have months before that happens. Let's give it a few more weeks."

"No. We did things your way, but it's not working."

"How about one more week? We're outside of a travel lane, and nothing is out this way. It will take time for that shuttle to fly wherever it went and bring another one back."

"The other clone could have sent a transmission and stayed at this location if he didn't plan to abandon us for good." He crossed his arms over his chest, his expression stubborn.

Her temper was beginning to rise. "Are you serious? And say what? The woman who helped us escape Clone World is waiting at this location with four clones. Please haul ass there to speak to her. Oh, and if anyone is listening, which is highly likely, this is exactly where we are."

He scowled.

"That kind of conversation being broadcast would get the authorities motivated to come after us. You know how terrified humans are of clones. They've fucked our kind over in every way imaginable by giving us zero rights or considerations. It's a miracle there haven't been rebellions. They know it, too. It's why they panic at just the thought of clones running around free."

MC-3 approached, placing her hands on the tall male. "Marisol has a point. We should give it at least another week. It would be best if we find the other clones that escaped. They can help us learn how to survive since they've been doing it for years."

He glared down at the female. "I didn't ask you."

She jerked her hands away and glared back at him. "You are not in charge, and I have a say in the matter. We all do."

MC-2 and MC-3 nodded.

"Fine, we'll vote," MC-1 stated. "Raise your hand if you believe it's best if we go find an uninhabited planet to live on."

Marisol couldn't stay silent. "That means going to a planet humans deemed too terrible to try to live on. So horrific storms, animals that will kill us, or something is terribly wrong with the environment. Like the air is barely breathable or the gravity is so strong it will mess up our bodies."

MC-1 sneered at her but didn't say a word. He did raise his hand, though. No one else did.

The muscle in his jaw clenched. "Raise your hand if you believe we should wait for what I'm starting to doubt anyone is going to come meet with us."

Marisol and the other three clones raised their hands. She didn't miss how quickly the dynamics had changed since they'd left Clone World. The four medics had gone from taking orders from her to using a voting system.

"You're fools!" MC-1 stomped toward the back of the shuttle. There was cargo storage and a bathroom for him to step into if he wanted some alone time.

Once he was gone, Marisol forced a smile at the other three. "Thank you for agreeing with me. I—"

A loud beeping cut her off. Marisol bolted toward the front of the shuttle and entered the cockpit. The alarm going off showed that something had shown up on long-range sensors. A vessel was coming from the direction of the Balarian system.

MC-3 stepped next to her. "It's the authorities, isn't it?"

"I don't think so. They'd be traveling from Vista's system. That's the closest base they have in this sector of space. Clone World doesn't allow them to keep a base there. My gramps doesn't want Earth keeping an eye on what's going on there. That ship might be who we've been waiting for."

"Hail them," MC-2 hissed. "Find out."

Two more vessels showed up on sensors coming from another direction. There were no known space stations or colonized planets that way. Both were traveling close enough together, making her hope it was Figures and Free.

More beeping signaled yet another vessel coming within sensor range. It was coming from another part of space that was known for nothing being out there. The vessels were far enough away that the readings weren't very clear about their models or class. They could be a freighter, a transport, or a shuttle. The only thing for certain was that none of them were huge enough to be a pleasure cruiser.

"The authorities have come to kill us!" MC-3 rushed out of the cockpit, fleeing toward the back.

"Is that what is happening?" MC-4 crouched down next to Marisol, her eyes huge with fear. "Did the other pilot you spoke to turn us in?"

"Figures wouldn't do that." Marisol ran deeper scans. More information came in. "They are all shuttles." She frowned. "Neither of the two seemingly traveling together have the same configuration as the previous shuttle we had contact with."

"What does that mean?"

Marisol started to buckle into the pilot seat. "I'm not sure, but I want you all to belt in."

"You believe they've all come to capture or kill us." MC-2 threw himself in the other seat, grabbed MC-4, and yanked her onto his lap. He began strapping them both in.

Marisol went over her options. She could make a run for it but it was possible that one of those incoming shuttles was Free. It was a huge risk, but she started the engines and sent out a general communication hail, hoping to find out who was flying those other shuttles.

Seconds ticked into almost a minute before there was a response. It was coming from the farthest away shuttle heading at her. She opened a channel.

"Alpha, Roger form, line six. The two incomings are slightly spaced apart. Do you understand?"

That voice belonged to Figures. At least, she was almost certain that it was him. A.R. forms on Clone World were for stolen property losses.

Line six meant a group of thieves. Marisol stared at the two close-together blips on her sensors. He was implying they were pirates.

"Are you sure?" Marisol wanted verification.

"Affirmative. Red, nine, seven, zero, bar, ten." He took a breath. "Seven, seven, seven on the other inbound."

Marisol felt terror. R970B10 was the accounting budget they used for everything from security on Clone World planet to the massive ground cannons that could take down vessels trying to land or take off from the surface.

Was he telling her to fight if she needed to? To open fire on the advancing two shuttles if they tried to dock with her? He also wanted her to wait for further input.

No. He's telling me that the other ship is probably Free. Or at least another clone.

"Understood." She wanted clarification, though. "Are you saying nine, six, zero?" That would be the first three numbers for weapon purchases.

"Nine, six, zero. Confirmed."

She ended the communications and brought the weapons for the shuttle online. Insecurity was a terrible thing to feel. The few piloting lessons she'd taken over the years left her ill-equipped to fight a battle. Those pilots sure hadn't done more than give her a general rundown of how the weapons system could protect the shuttle if the need ever arose.

MC-1 suddenly rushed inside the cockpit, slightly out of breath. "Three said we're being surrounded. Get us out of here!"

Marisol was in no mood to deal with him. "Shut up, go in the back, and strap in. We have two pirate shuttles inbound, but two more shuttles are the clones we came looking for. I don't have time to argue with you. I need to learn the weapons system."

"You need to learn? Don't you know how to use them already?" MC-1 seemed outraged as he shouted.

"I'm not an actual pilot. It would have been too suspicious if I'd asked anyone to teach me how to target and fire on other shuttles. I made it seem like I wanted to learn how to fly a shuttle for the fun of it. So yes, I need to learn how to use the weapons system. Go in the back."

"Do it," MC-2 barked. "Listen to Marisol. You're not helping. Fill a few syringes with plasma in case the human pirates are able to dock and board our shuttle. That's how you can help."

Marisol inwardly flinched overhearing that. Clone plasma injected into humans would cause their deaths. It had been a possibility that they might have to kill or be killed. She just had hoped it wouldn't come down to that. It seemed like it might be the case.

She didn't protest that drastic defensive plan, memorizing the weapons controls instead. They had seven laser cannons mounted on the shuttle exterior and eight missiles. That didn't seem like a lot to her.

Marisol really hoped that the shuttle coming from the Balarian system was Free. Not that she should be thinking about him right then. Their lives were on the line.

Please be him. I hope he still loves me.

The two inbound pirate shuttles were bearing down on them fast. She made a split-second decision, hit the thrusters, changed course, and flew toward the shuttle she hoped Free was on. All she could do was pray that whoever was flying it knew how to fight off pirates and they'd save her and the four medics.

* * * * *

Free ignored that his engines were running hot and that the shuttle exceeded the safe speed parameters. He'd been in a daze for the past three and a half days since he'd been in contact with Figures and Big. They'd given him the shock of his life by saying that Marisol was looking for him.

Memories replayed through his head, tormenting him ever since. Marisol Florigo should have been everything he was supposed to hate. She was human. Also, the granddaughter of the man who'd enslaved his kind, buying and treating clones as if they were nothing more than mindless products.

She even stood to inherit ownership of Clone World one day if Rico Florigo allowed himself to die and stay dead. He highly doubted that was the case. Free had seen and learned too much about the old human over the years he'd been trapped on Clone World.

The proof of how cruel, calculating, and malicious Rico Florigo could be had been constant. Free had seen it by how the old human had reacted when a guest murdered a clone. The killers weren't prosecuted for their crimes. They were billed hefty fees and replacement charges instead.

The old man bought unblanked clones knowing they'd go insane and have short, miserable lives. Rico Florigo had built a lucrative business on the suffering and exploitation of clones. The bastard was proud of the immense wealth he'd amassed with their blood, sweat, and tears. Even their brutal deaths at times.

Marisol wasn't anything like her grandfather. That's what Free had quickly learned working with her. They'd spent at least six days a week, hours each day, in close proximity, going over budgets, profit and loss statements, and purchasing orders for Clone World.

She didn't treat him the way other humans did. They were cold, demanding, and insulting. Some went out of their way to anger him, hoping for a reaction. That would have meant immediate termination. Death was the consequence of an aggressive or insolent clone. No exceptions were made. They weren't even permitted to defend themselves if a human attacked. Clones were supposed to just take whatever abuse was dealt, even if it meant certain death.

Marisol was kind, considerate, and even funny when they were alone. She made Free feel seen and heard for the first time in his life. His ideas were welcomed, and she encouraged him to help her run the finance department. She saw him as a person.

She'd also shown him absolute trust by sending the human guards out of the room while they were working closely together. The other human employees he'd had meetings with never did that. They ordered an armed guard to remain within eyesight, watching his every move. He knew they feared him and worried that a clone might snap and harm them.

Marisol had treated him as if they were equals. There was no way he could have avoided falling in love with her. She had become the center of his world. He lived for her smiles, teasing jokes, and the warm look in her soulful brown eyes.

She had a heart-shaped face and kissable-looking lips he longed to taste, and she always kept her light brown hair in a tight bun. He had been excited the first time she'd worn it down and free. The tresses fell like a silky curtain to her shoulders. It had tormented him a little since he'd wanted to feel the texture to see if it was as soft as it looked.

He'd spent every evening laying on his bunk, wishing they could spend time together outside the office. It was impossible, of course. That didn't mean Free hadn't fantasized about taking Marisol on picnics or to one of the fancy restaurants the guests dined at.

Humans dated. Free had dreamed about all the activities he'd like to do with Marisol. She deserved to be romanced. He'd gone so far as to spy on some of the guests with the help of a security clone giving access to the live feeds. He'd wanted to learn how to dance by watching couples do that activity. It would give him a valid reason to hold Marisol in his arms.

Clones weren't permitted to have sex and shouldn't even have those types of thoughts. His nutrient bars were laced with certain drugs to keep those urges from happening. Every three months, he had medical checkups when he was given plasma. Hormone levels were tested as part of the exam.

His had been erratic after spending so much time with Marisol. Not high enough to justify a chemical increase, but he'd begun to suffer from having erections. That wasn't supposed to be possible for someone like him. He was an F Clone. His duties didn't put him in contact with any human guests. Some of them paid extra to see a male stripped to view a clone penis. He'd heard horror stories about that being done occasionally from the males who shared his bunk room.

Free also had begun to have sexual dreams about Marisol. Just the idea of kissing her, getting her bare, and exploring her body had him hacking into databases to learn more about the topic of sex. The guests were given access to something called porn videos. He'd watched a few of them, so he'd be able to please her in bed if ever given the opportunity.

Marisol Florigo was forbidden to him in every way. Yet he'd still fallen in love. Over time, she seemed to start having those same feelings for him. She'd reach out to brush her hand over his. There were comments she'd made about how she thought he was handsome and attractive. Every wonderful word she had spoken only encouraged him to fall deeper in love with her.

She'd been the one to bring up escaping Clone World. It had been impossible for them to be together if they remained on the planet. Security was too tight. The few stolen moments they had were inside the office. At any given time, there were half a dozen human guards nearby. All of them stuck close to Marisol or checked on her every few minutes. The best they could do were a few hugs, some swift kisses, and whispered private words.

Free was an F Clone, which only gave him access to the housing he'd been assigned and the finance department. His knowledge of classified information kept him highly isolated. Human security officers escorted him from one building to the other every day. Even the clones he shared a bunk room all worked in other highly restricted areas.

Leaving Marisol behind when he'd escaped Clone World with five other clones had been one of the most difficult things he'd ever done. She had insisted she couldn't go with them, certain her grandfather would go to any lengths to have them hunted and captured. Rico Florigo would see his granddaughter being with a lowly clone as the ultimate betrayal.

Her plan was to leave later. That way, she wouldn't be linked to the clones' escape. The two months they'd planned to be apart had seemed excruciatingly long. Free had no idea their plans wouldn't work out, or he'd have stayed behind to be with her. His main motivation for leaving had always been for them to be together.

His heart had felt ripped from his chest when they'd flown to Barlish station and waited for Marisol to contact them. She was supposed to bribe someone there to put her in an emergency pod and eject it into space. Then they would have maneuvered their shuttle to catch it inside their cargo hold. Marisol would have been reunited with him.

The hours had turned to days of silence. No message from Marisol had come. Security on Barlish was too tight for them to attempt to dock and physically search for her. All sections of the station had scanners that automatically read every person coming or going. Clones didn't have chips embedded in their palms. Security would have immediately realized they weren't human and arrested them. Death would have swiftly followed.

All six of them had attempted to use their unique hacking skills to breach the station's security office to gain information about Marisol, but it had been a completely closed system with no weaknesses to find. It had taken nine days before the other clones had convinced Free that Marisol wouldn't be joining them.

Free had been heartbroken at first, but as the months passed, he'd become certain that something had gone wrong. Marisol loved him, and he refused to believe she'd changed her mind.

It had motivated him to be the first of their group of six clones to leave the home base they'd created on the mining station. He'd gained their help to steal a shuttle for his private use. The first solo mission he'd taken had been extremely dangerous. He'd flown close enough to Clone World, attempting to establish contact with Marisol. He'd failed.

Three years had passed, his heart battered, and his soul darkened with misery over her loss. The future they'd envisioned hadn't come to pass. Then he'd gotten the communication from Big and Figures. Marisol had left Clone World and was on a shuttle trying to find him.

Free's heart raced as soon as a shuttle showed on his sensors near an asteroid belt and moon that Figures called his secondary home. Marisol was on that shuttle. He couldn't wait to see her, speak with her, and find out if she still had feelings for him.

Unfortunately, two more vessels immediately showed on the sensors. He knew they weren't his fellow clones from the direction they were flying from. Blade had been captured by pirates and held against his will for a long time by them. One of their hubs came from that direction. Pirates were after his Marisol.

"I'll kill you all before I allow you to harm her," he snarled.

The shuttle that had to be Marisol's suddenly moved, turned in his direction, and began flying right toward him. His Marisol knew he'd keep her safe. It warmed his soul thinking that she was depending on him to save her.

"I will," he vehemently swore.

Chapter Six

Marisol focused on the shuttle she approached. It was in clear view now, and she identified it as a personal cruiser class shuttle. It was a popular model for people who lived amongst the stars instead of on planets.

The other two shuttles that she felt certain were pirates were gaining on her. That terrified her. The communications beeped.

"Answer it," MC-2 demanded.

She didn't even spare him or the female clone on his lap a glance as she opened the channel.

"Cease running and shut down your engines, or we'll fire on you," a man demanded. "Comply or die."

The signal was coming from one of the two pirate shuttles. Marisol bit her lip, debating on whether she should say anything back. Alarms blared on her console, warning her that someone had a weapons lock on them. Terror coursed through her.

"Let them board us," MC-2 whispered. "We'll defend ourselves. They can only dock one shuttle to ours. We're five against however many they have. I'm sure we'll overpower them, and then we can take control of their ship."

"Another shuttle isn't going to do us any good since I'm the only one who knows how to fly. I'd also not like them to get that close to us. Did you ever consider that they might have illegal weapons? You have no idea how quickly those can kill us." Marisol didn't want to frighten them, but they'd been shielded from reality by living on Clone World with their heavy security protocols.

MC-4 whimpered.

Another alarm blasted through the cockpit, and Marisol watched in shock as the shuttle they approached, the one she felt Free might be on, was the one to launch a weapon. A missile flew past them.

"Brace for sharp maneuvers," she yelled out. Then Marisol pushed the engines for all they had, trying to put more distance between her and the pirates. She didn't see the missile hit, but it showed on her sensors.

One of the hostile shuttles veered off from pursuit, parts of it breaking apart. The other hostile shuttle fired on them.

Warning alarms blared again, and Marisol responded by changing course. The missile coming at them missed, but it was close. It exploded, though, scattering large chunks of debris. They couldn't avoid some of it.

Damage reports started scrolling across her screen, red lights flashed inside the cockpit, and engine one died. It sent the shuttle into a spin, causing her to lose control. They were rolling, and the view out of the cockpit window showed other shuttles, but then there was utter blackness.

Marisol quickly compensated by cutting the second engine and using thrusters. The gravity stabilizers went off-line. The sudden weightlessness made her feel queasy. She got the spin under control, so their view wasn't constantly changing.

"Engine one refuses to restart," Marisol updated the clones. "It's too damaged. I've got enough thruster control that we've straightened out."

Her fingers flew over the console. "The gravity stabilizers are refusing to reboot."

"Life support is online but flashing a warning," MC-2 shared, reading the system alerts from the other console where he sat.

"I don't have time to worry about that," Marisol admitted. Her gaze went to the two shuttles that had engaged in firing at each other. Her sensors read that the damaged pirate shuttle was floating away, seeming to have lost all power. The important thing was it wasn't anywhere near them.

"Reboot all the systems," MC-2 ordered.

"No. I'm using the thrusters to keep us away from the battle. Rebooting would knock out all systems for at least a full minute. We can't afford to take any more damage."

Her gaze went to the long-range sensors. The farthest away shuttle, the one Free had to be on, appeared to be undamaged. He had the other pirate ship on the run. The one incoming shuttle that she felt Figures might be on split into two separate vessels as she watched. They flew close together, but one of them broke away to fly faster.

Marisol was stunned since that fifth one hadn't been on sensors before. "Where the hell did that come from, and who is it?"

"We're going to die," MC-4 sniffed.

Marisol glanced toward the couple strapped in the other seat. The female clone was crying. Her male was doing something to the console on that side. It alarmed her. "Do not reboot the systems."

"Life support went down," he grimly shared.

"We have enough oxygen to breathe for a bit." Marisol had to make things clear so he wouldn't interfere. "Right now, we need to worry about not taking more damage, or we're dead. That means I need working thrusters in case we need to move."

Marisol watched as the two battling shuttles fired on each other. The pirate ship suddenly changed course, but instead of heading toward Marisol's crippled shuttle, it flew toward the second one, aimlessly floating.

Free, or who she thought was him, broke away and changed course toward her. He put his shuttle between her and the two pirate ones. Marisol had maneuvered her shuttle away enough that it would take him a few minutes to reach them. A glance at communications showed it was down. No one could try to talk to them.

The pirate ship seemed to spear the damaged one with a harpoon-like cable and started to haul it back in the direction they'd originally come from. Relief flooded through Marisol. "The pirates are fleeing!"

Her gaze went to the incoming unknown shuttle that had popped up on sensors without warning, hoping it wasn't someone who meant them harm. It was reading as a Varlius class. Those were top-of-the-line luxury shuttles.

"That other shuttle is slowing. I think it's planning on docking with us."

"I see, MC-2." Marisol wished the comms still worked. She did shut down thrusters. As soon as that happened, all power went out. Everything on the console flickered before it completely died.

"What is happening?" MC-4 loudly sobbed now.

"Calm down," Marisol ordered. It was terrifying and eerie sitting in a dead cockpit with no power. She couldn't see anything. The only sounds came from the panicking female clone.

Marisol blindly felt the console, reached under it, and felt for the cap. It was located a little to her left. She slid it open and flipped the switch. It was the emergency backup control to reboot all systems.

Nothing happened for what felt like an entirety, but in reality, it was probably a full minute. Then pale yellow lights blinked on the console. Red flashing lights came on overhead next. More power surged into the console, but a lot of systems remained down. That included long-range sensors and communications.

"Life support is still reading as down," MC-2 ground out.

"I see that." It didn't take Marisol long to figure out they were in deep trouble. Both engines were reading non-operational. The thrusters weren't responding. Life support was down. The only good news was that they weren't showing a hull breach. They might be dead in space, but the shuttle wasn't coming apart.

Marisol reached for her belts, releasing them. "Stay here. The entire system is rebooting." She didn't mention that she was sure it wouldn't do any good.

It was difficult to move without gravity as she floated out of her seat. The cockpit doors were wide open since they never sealed them off. She had to grip the seat she'd just left and use it to push off against, floating toward the back.

More red flashing lighting from the ceiling bathed the living area of the shuttle. MC-1 and MC-3 were strapped onto the couch. Both silently stared at her. They each held one of their med kits on their laps.

"We are probably about to be boarded," she told them.

MC-1 growled, rage twisting his features. He fumbled with the kit, probably to get a syringe ready.

Marisol shook her head. "I don't think they are hostile. It might be Free. Don't you dare attack him."

"Why is gravity out?"

"We've lost most systems. I started a complete reboot, but engine one showed severe damage before we lost power. The gravity stabilizers probably are too damaged to come back online." Marisol floated by them, lightly bumped against the ceiling, and grabbed hold of one of the strips to pull herself along toward the very back of the shuttle. "Just remain buckled in. I'm going to the cargo hold where I think the other shuttle will dock with us."

"You think?" MC-1 started to unbuckle. "I'm coming with you."

"Fucking stay there." Marisol didn't trust him not to attack Free or whoever was in that shuttle that had come for them. "I've got this."

Something hit the shuttle. The impact was enough to tear her away from the ceiling and send her weightless body careening into a wall. She hit it with a grunt of pain but grabbed hold of another wall strip to prevent her body from bouncing away from the side.

One thing became increasingly clear to Marisol. It was hard to move about without gravity in the cabin. It was also an experience she hoped never to repeat. She'd spent her entire life living on a planet. The space travel trips she'd taken for business had always been necessary, but then again, she'd never been inside a damaged shuttle before. It was terrible.

An alarm sounded from the back. It was probably a warning that someone had attached to the docking doors. Marisol pulled herself toward the cargo area again. It was slow going since she had no experience dealing with being weightless. She almost made it to the doorway at the back section when it suddenly opened.

The sight that met her gaze had Marisol freeze in place. The lighting was bad since only red flashing lights washed over the face of the man who braced upright in the doorway. It was enough, though, for Marisol to open gawk at a face she had thought she'd never see again. It was Free.

His blond hair was cut short, accenting his masculine bone structure. A black body suit stretched tautly over his muscled arms, wide shoulders, and dense chest. He'd filled out since she'd last seen him. She identified the outfit he wore as a popular space suit. Only he wasn't wearing the matching helmet.

"Marisol," he rasped.

He suddenly used his grip on the open doorway to thrust his body forward, coming right at her.

"Free!" Tears blinded Marisol as she released the wall. "It's really you!"

His much bigger body floated at her, his gloved hands gripping her before they roughly collided, and he yanked her tight against his chest. She felt them turn in the air as Free wrapped his body around hers. They hit something, him taking the brunt of the impact, but his hold on her didn't loosen.

Marisol clung to him, burying her face against his exposed throat. Emotion muted her as she fought back the urge to sob. It was really Free. He was alive, holding her, and they'd found each other again.

"I was afraid to believe it when Big and Fig told me you were out here." He held her tighter.

"I died," she blurted out. "That's why I wasn't able to get off Barlish station and meet up with you."

"What?" He used his hold on her to pull back until their faces were inches apart.

"I died. I just didn't know it. I'm a clone. My gramps didn't even tell me what happened or what he'd had done to me. I only found out recently and started immediately plotting our escape from Clone World."

His shock was clear as his beautiful blue eyes widened.

"I thought you changed your mind about being with me when I didn't get a message that you were waiting for me to escape my security detail and eject in a pod you could pick up. I died just hours after reaching Barlish, and my body got shipped to Earth for an unblanked body to be grown," she told him.

He studied her features, staying nothing.

She felt a little fear. "Does it matter to you that I'm a clone now?"

"No. We were there waiting for you to contact us. I thought you'd changed your mind."

"I would never do that. All I wanted was to be with you. Free..." She burst into tears and lunged, hugging him tight again and burying her face back into the warm skin of his neck. All Marisol wanted to do was cling to him and never let go.

"I have you," Free whispered in her ear. "We're together now. No one and nothing will keep us apart."

"Excuse me," MC-1 interrupted. "I take it that you're a clone?"

Free tensed against Marisol.

"They are clones, too," she muttered against his skin, breathing him in and still not wanting to let go. "My medical team of four was assigned to care for me. Two more are in the cockpit. I had to take them with me, or Gramps probably would have killed them in a fit of rage after he realized I'd escaped."

Free kept hold of her but shifted his head, probably to get a better look at the two clones strapped to the couch. "Yes. I'm an F Clone, formally known as Freak. You may call me Free. That's the name I go by now."

Marisol didn't bother to look at the clones Free was speaking to. She really didn't care how they reacted as long as they didn't attack. They didn't.

Free squeezed Marisol. "We have to leave right now. The pirates sent out a hail with clicking sounds."

"What does that mean?" Marisol didn't understand.

"I think it's a language or code they use to avoid drawing attention from the authorities in the next system. I saw the damage to your shuttle as I docked with you. We need to abandon it and go on my shuttle now. Time isn't on our side. More pirates will be coming."

"You seemed to have kicked their ass. Why would they come back?"

Marisol felt irritated with MC-1. It wasn't his place to question Free. Yet...he was.

"We're out of normal shipping lanes, and they will be desperate to steal shuttle parts and cargo from us." Free patiently explained. "The pirates just underestimated us by only bringing two teams to attack. More will be coming. We need to leave."

Marisol hated letting him go, but she understood the danger. "We brought plasma."

"I saw two stasis pods. Are more clones inside them?"

"No." Marisol pulled back finally, enough to look at Free's handsome face. She couldn't get enough of seeing him. "They are just part of a ruse we used to escape Clone World. Do you have a use for them?"

"No. Leave the pods." Free turned his head, staring at the two clones on the couch. He raised his voice. "Grab what you can and head toward my shuttle. We need to be gone in two minutes."

"Who are you?"

Marisol twisted her head, seeing MC-2 floating near the open cockpit door. "We don't have time for explanations. More pirates are inbound. Grab one of the plasma crates from the cargo bay. We're switching shuttles. This is Free. He's the clone I told you about."

MC-2 gave a sharp nod. "What about our food and clothing?"

"Leave them," Free ordered. "Those things can be easily replaced. I have plenty to share on my shuttle."

Chapter Seven

Free couldn't stop staring and touching Marisol. She was real and finally with him again. The things she'd told him in the minutes he'd been with her were shocking. She had died, and her grandfather had her made into an unblanked clone. He couldn't imagine how much internal trauma she'd suffered upon learning that.

Four clones were traveling with her, two males and two females. That didn't surprise him. Marisol had always had a big heart and didn't look down on clones the way other humans did. She knew they had emotions and feelings. Their lives mattered. The woman he'd fallen in love with wouldn't have willingly left them behind to die.

"We need to transfer over to my shuttle immediately," he stated loudly so everyone understood. "More pirates will be coming. Your shuttle is too damaged to fly, and we don't have time to haul it back to our home base. We'll leave it behind to give the pirates an alternative target to focus on."

He pulled Marisol toward the cargo hold where he'd docked their shuttles together. He didn't care about the plasma they'd brought along. They had plenty stored back on the mining station. The important thing was getting them to safety. It was slower going since gravity wasn't present in the damaged shuttle.

"Move quickly," Free called out. He spotted strapped-down boxes, noticing they were marked as 'files.' "Do you need anything from in here?" He stared into Marisol's deep brown eyes. "We can't come back to retrieve any items once we abandon this shuttle. The pirates will take it."

"I have a bag over there." She pointed to a black suitcase. "It has some of my important mementos I didn't want to leave behind."

"I'll grab it."

"Thank you. It's some things that belonged to my parents and a few of my favorite childhood toys. I was too afraid to pack them when I went to meet with you the first time. It's a good thing I didn't take them then, or they'd have been lost when I died."

He hated to release her but did, pushing her toward the open docking sleeve. "Be careful when you transition inside my shuttle. Gravity is stable there. I'll get your case." He used the wall to push off, aiming for the far corner.

One of the male clones entered the cargo hold, frowning at Free. He appeared wary and unsure of what to do or say.

Free didn't have that problem. "Grab whatever you want to take with us, and be careful when you enter my shuttle. I wasn't aware you'd lost gravity, so I didn't turn my stabilizer off. The first step into my cargo hold will be difficult as you transition."

"Can we trust you?"

Free didn't have time to hold a discussion with the male. "I'm a clone. Either come with us or die. The pirates might not kill you, but they will enslave you. They already did that to one of us who recently was able to escape their clutches. We'll sit down and talk later."

That seemed to mollify him. The male medic clone floated to a box and began to unstrap it. The two females and the last male floated into the cargo hold. All three of them appeared confused and disorientated.

"Grab a box or just enter my shuttle. We're out of here in one minute. More pirates are coming. Move if you want to stay alive and free." Free hoped that would motivate them not to waste time.

"I just left the cockpit," the second male stated, staring at him. "I don't see any new signals showing on long-range sensors."

"Not yet, but they will be coming," Free assured him. "It's what they do." He got the suitcase Marisol had wanted free and gripped it by the handle, using the wall to push against. He aimed for the open docking door.

"Stay or go, but I'm leaving. I strongly suggest you come with us," Free told them. His heart wasn't soft like Marisol's. They'd either decide to live or allow their stupidity and naivety to get them killed. Marisol was already on board. She was Free's priority.

The transition from the other shuttle to his was brutal as Free staggered, almost dropping the now-heavy suitcase. His body had been light, but now gravity made movement extremely awkward for the first few steps.

Marisol was in his cargo hold, leaning against the wall for support. Her features were strained, and she appeared to be in some pain. He didn't see any blood or other injuries. That didn't mean she hadn't somehow gotten hurt.

Free strode to her, put the suitcase down, and attached the handle to a strap. It was the quickest way to secure it in the hold. "Are you alright? What happened?"

"I collapsed when I stepped into gravity. I'm fine, though. I just really banged up my knees and will probably have some bruising."

"I warned you to be careful. I didn't find you, only for something bad to happen to you, Marisol."

She gave him an unsteady smile. "I tried to be careful. It's not like you can really prepare for how drastic the difference is, though, when you've never experienced something like that before."

"True." Free rose to his full height, turning when there was a loud thump. One of the female clones lay sprawled over one of the boxes she'd been carrying. She groaned as she tried to stand up. Gravity seemed to make that impossible.

Free moved quickly to her side, bent over, and pulled her up. He released her just as quickly. "Move slowly until you adjust to not being weightless anymore," he instructed. Then he yelled at the other three clones. "Hurry up. Get out of there. We need to go."

The other three stumbled, and two dropped their boxes as they entered his cargo hold. Free felt sympathy for them, knowing being in space exposed them to a lot of new experiences they weren't really prepared for. He sealed his side of the docking door.

"Tightly secure those boxes down and then find a seat to belt into." Free turned, strode to Marisol, and easily swept her into his arms. "I don't want you walking until we're sure it's not more than bruising from your fall."

The hug he'd gotten from her had been great, but cradling Marisol in his arms as he moved through his shuttle toward the cockpit was even better. Especially when she wrapped her arms around his neck.

He inhaled, picking up her clean scent. It was still messing with his mind that Marisol was really there. He'd dreamed of them being together far too many times and then been tormented when that plan had fallen through.

"What is the mental status of the clones you brought with you?" He needed to know if they posed any threat. "Be blunt."

"MC-1 is the dominant one of their group and has started to give me a lot of pushback. Nothing serious, though. He is just very opinionated and questions everything. It's mostly annoying."

"Has he given you any trouble or gotten physical?" Free gently deposited her into the co-pilot seat. He wanted to keep Marisol close and within eyesight.

One glance back through the open doors revealed that only one of the female clones had entered the living space. The other three were probably still securing the boxes they'd carried aboard in the cargo hold.

"No. MC-1 hasn't touched me or made me feel afraid of him."

Free was glad to hear that. It would be traumatic if he had to kill one of the clones after she'd gone to the trouble to save them. He dropped into his seat, using the controls to undock the damaged shuttle. He also sealed the cockpit doors, locking them inside.

Marisol twisted in her seat and glanced back before frowning at him. "Why did you seal us inside alone? I'm sure the M's are scared and want assurances that everything is going to be okay."

"I don't have the time or patience to answer questions from them or establish that I'm in charge right now."

"I understand. Maybe I should go back there just so they aren't alone. It will comfort them."

"They aren't children." Once again she was proving to Free that she had a soft heart and saw clones as equals.

"In a way, they are. They were segregated from other clones because they were the medical team assigned to my care. I've learned a lot from them since we left Clone World."

Free was listening as he prepared to fly them to safety. He loved the sound of her voice. So much so that he wanted to hear her talk more. "Tell me."

"They weren't assigned to a high-security bunk room the way you were. My grandfather had them living in an isolated cottage off the beaten path. Every delivery made to them was through robotic drones. They were only allowed to speak to each other. My gramps sent them electronic orders, so they didn't even get to speak directly to him."

"They had contact with you."

"No, they didn't. Not in the way you think. The housing staff contacted them after dosing my food with a drug that would put me to sleep. They came in an hour after I ate and gave me plasma after I was unconscious."

Rage filled him. "Your food was drugged?"

"Yes. I wasn't thrilled about finding that out either, but it was the only way for me to be given transfusions without knowing I'd been turned into a clone. It seems Gramps had told my housing staff that he was having them drug me so security could search my home for electronic listening devices. At least, that's what the M's assumed from the messages they received about how I should be asleep and wouldn't know they were there to protect my privacy from being invaded."

"The housing staff didn't know the truth?"

"I assume not. Just...be nice to them, please. They took good care of me when I didn't even know it."

"I hear you and understand what you're saying. Those four clones will be fine for now. I want you to stay close to me where I know you're safe."

He finished assessing the current situation. Blade's Varlius class vessel floated next to him, but Figures had flown to place his shuttle between him and the retreating pirates. A quick check revealed that they were still broadcasting a strange clicking-sounding signal.

Free knew in his gut it was definitely a coded message calling for assistance from their hub. He opened communications to let Blade and Figures know they were ready to leave. They also needed to know he planned to abandon the other shuttle.

Blade spoke before he could. "Our brother flew to that spot to get better sensor readings and is picking up five incoming. We need to go. What is the condition of the CL?"

Free understood that Blade was asking about the shuttle from Clone World. Five incoming would mean additional pirate ships with more teams of thieves. "It's too damaged to worry about. I've got what we came for. What extraction plan was decided on?"

"V formation. I'm the lead. You're port side. Follow me."

"Understood." Free didn't need his thrusters to put distance between his vessel and the one they'd just abandoned. The clones hadn't known to close the cargo door on it as they'd left, and he hadn't cared what had happened to the other shuttle. The oxygen venting from it had already separated them as soon as he'd severed their connection.

"Buckle in," he ordered Marisol. It took effort for him to fly the shuttle when all he wanted to do was stare at her. Touch her. Talk to her and find out more about what happened to her. He was also curious what her life had been like while they'd been apart.

First he needed to get them all to safety and back at the mining station that they'd turned into their home base. Part of him suddenly worried that she might not like it there. It was a problem to deal with later. Just like the four clones Marisol had brought with her. It was a good thing that more clones had escaped, but it would have been bad if they hadn't integrated well with others.

He followed Blade, keeping on the left side and behind the larger shuttle. They picked up speed when Figures joined them, flying in a direction that didn't take them directly to their destination. They couldn't risk the pirates tracking them.

"You look really good."

Free tensed, turning his head. Marisol's normally restrained light brown hair hung longer than the last time he'd seen it down. Those times were few. Her dark eyes locked on him, making him want to get closer.

He forced himself to look away. "You are beyond beautiful."

"Why are you barely speaking and looking at me? Did your feelings change? Did you find someone else?"

"No!" He clenched his teeth, adjusting course when Blade did.

"Then why do you seem to be doing your best to ignore me? I have so much to say to you. I want to hear everything that I've missed out on. A thousand questions are filling my head."

"I would like nothing better than to take you to my cabin and lock us in there so nothing could disturb us. I have dreamed about you every time I slept. Missed you." He sucked in a deep breath. "But now isn't the time. I dropped everything the second Big and Figures let me know you were looking for me. I stressed my engines to reach you quickly, not caring if I burned them out and lost the use of my shuttle in the end. This has been my home ever since I left the others."

"Then—"

He cut her off. "Do you know what pirates would do to you? You're a female. They would..." He cleared his throat, not wanting to voice such vile things. "I'm not allowing that to happen. I will take you home where it's safe, and then it will be our time to reconnect."

Marisol sighed. "Okay. You're being logical. I've missed that about you. Honestly, I've missed everything about you, Free. I dreamed about you, too. I thought you had changed your mind about being with me when you didn't send me that signal you'd be there to catch me when I ejected from the station."

"We were there." He changed course again, keeping in the flying formation Blade led. It was important to make certain the pirates couldn't follow them or even guess the correct direction they'd gone.

The mining station was well protected, but it was best to never put their defenses to the test. Some pirate hubs were known to have hundreds of criminals living together. They would attack if they ever realized what was hidden deep inside the crater they called home. The pirates would want to not only steal every resource the mining company had abandoned but probably take it over themselves.

"We sent dozens of messages, but you never responded."

"I never got them because I was already dead."

His guts twisted. "Don't say that."

"It's true. Original me was killed. Gramps obviously had some fake memories implanted because I vaguely remember attending some meetings, then feeling super sick, and later attributed it to being severely depressed when you never showed up."

"I am here now, aren't I?" It angered him that she'd believe he would abandon her. "I came for you then, too. I will *always* come for you."

He didn't dare look her way, knowing he'd revealed the depth of his feelings. They'd never faded. Marisol had earned his heart and devotion in the past. It was the reason he'd grown distant from the other clones after believing he'd lost her forever. Free had struggled to find a reason to go on without her. Big, Blade, Figures, Ram, and Rod had never understood his almost obsession with Marisol. They'd never been in love.

"Who is the female unblanked clone you ordered?" She hesitated. "I randomly checked that secret account we put money into and saw the payment made to DJD Clone Corp."

"I don't have many details. We must speak in code over long-distance communications so no one can guess who and what we are. Big let me know that Figures had met a woman that he wanted to make a part of our family and was paying for her transportation from our old savings account."

Marisol remained silent.

He glanced her way. She silently watched him, a small frown turning the corners of her mouth downward. He started to explain how they communicated.

"The words we use are always important hints. Figures wanted to make her, paired with a part of our family, let me fill in the gaps that he was paying for an unblanked clone to be made of whoever that human had been. I haven't gone home to the station in a long time. It was tempting to fly back to get more details, but knowing they'd used the funds from Clone World for something like that deeply angered me."

"I understand that. It never turns out well. Whoever was grown in the factory will go insane and die. I don't know what Figures was thinking doing something that terrible."

"That's not true. Big raided a transport for plasma and discovered one of your grandfather's private purchases onboard. She is not only surviving but also thriving as an unblanked clone." Free changed course again when Blade did. They were finally flying in the direction of the mining station. Nothing showed on long-range sensors. The pirates couldn't track them anymore.

"Then why were you mad?"

"I believed you'd made your choice to have nothing more to do with us. I took it as a personal betrayal that they'd take anything from you or your grandfather."

"Oh, Free..."

He swallowed down his bitter memories of how that had made him feel. "Now I know differently. I still don't think Figures should have used that money. We'll learn more once we reach home."

"Where is that? Do you live on a planet?"

It was tempting to change the subject. Clone World was a beautiful place despite the horrors of so many enslaved clones living there. The weather was always pleasant. The vegetation was plentiful and appealing to the eye. Marisol had grown up there. Now, all he could offer her was a station built inside a moon that used to belong to a mining company.

"Do you not want to tell me? Is it a surprise?"

He inhaled deeply. "I'm worried that you might hate it. It's not what you're used to."

"It's not Clone World. I'm sure I'll love it."

He glanced at Marisol, finding her staring at him with a small smile on her lips. He caved. "You deserve a beautiful planet, real sunshine, and fresh air. Unfortunately, that's not where our home base is located."

"You'll be there. That's all I need. Tell me."

"We thought about finding a planet after we escaped, but all research pointed to how difficult it would be to survive on any within range of us who still have access to plasma transports."

"You were stealing from the ones that got destroyed, right?"

"Yes." He adjusted course, keeping in formation with the other two shuttles. "We discovered a damaged and abandoned transport that was owned by a mining company. It might have contained food and water, so we boarded it. That's when we hacked into the mainframe computer, discovering it had originally come from a mining station that had been decommissioned. We went to check it out."

"And made it your home?"

"Yes. Our expectations were low that it would be salvageable for our needs, but it was so remote that the company didn't strip it. It was intact and just shut down."

"They probably didn't want to spend the money to have it torn apart and shipped anywhere."

He smiled. Marisol had always been quick with her mind. "That was our assumption, too. It was a large operation. There's even a shopping district. The stores had been looted a bit, but the storage rooms were full of merchandise. None of the humans tasked with closing the station down bothered to check them, or they didn't have the spare cargo room to empty them when they left."

"What kind of merchandise? I'm just curious."

"Everything you can imagine. Families lived there. One was a toy shop. That one wasn't looted. Dolls, trains, and everything a child could want are still displayed through the front windows."

"Really?" Marisol sounded amazed.

"Yes. I found it unsettling."

"Well, neither of us has been around children. Some come to Clone World with their parents, but most of them stay on whatever shuttles they arrive on with their nannies. It's not like the activities Gramps offers are geared toward underaged people."

"It reminds me that we'll never have children," he admitted.

Marisol didn't respond. Free turned his head, seeing her staring out the front window of the cockpit. She had a sad look on her face.

"What's wrong?"

She met his gaze. "I'm sorry that it was never an option for you. It's not fair. Gramps tried to talk me into having a baby right after my twenty-fifth birthday. I flat-out refused."

The emotion that filled him was one Free identified. Jealousy. "I didn't realize you were in love with someone before me."

"I wasn't. I mean, there wasn't someone special in my life. Do you really think I could be attracted to anyone who worked for my gramps? Or any of the guests who thought Clone World was a great place?" She shook her head. "The other men I met were at conferences. They were the competition or, worse, prospective clients."

"I worked for your grandfather."

"Not by choice. You know how the human staff treated you. All of them seemed to go out of their way to be rude and hateful toward clones, knowing there would be no reprisals. They relished that power."

"Why did you refuse? Did he pick a male to be the father that you couldn't stand?" He was curious.

"Growing up on Clone World was lonely and horrible for me. I wouldn't do that to someone else, especially my own baby. I had no friends, and I knew my gramps would manipulate and control them the way he always did with me. Employees have the option to quit and go live somewhere else if they hate him or being there. I literally had to escape to get out from under his thumb."

"I understand."

"How long is it going to take to reach this mining place?"

"Three days if we travel at top speed." He checked his engines. They were still running a little hot. He just hoped they held until they reached home base. The last thing he wanted was to have his shuttle break down while pirates were searching for them. He'd abandon it and have Blade transfer them all onto his fancy larger one. Marisol was the priority. Always.

A beeping started, and he realized Marisol's clones had figured out how to get his attention. At least one of them was attempting to enter the cockpit. They couldn't break in, but it would become annoying if they continued to push the button.

Chapter Eight

"What keeps beeping? Are the pirates showing up on your long-range sensors?"

Free wanted to growl. Marisol sounded worried. He didn't like that.

"No. One of your clones can't seem to figure out that I've locked the door and is repeatedly attempting to access the cockpit."

"I should go talk to them." Marisol started to unbuckle from her seat.

"No. I need to be the one to speak to them. Do you know how to fly one of these? You told me that you had a few pilots give you basic flying instructions."

"Yes. I'm the one who has been piloting the other shuttle since we left Clone World."

"Good. I'm transferring control to you. See how both of our shuttles are flying even with the wings of the biggest one? Blade is in front of us, and Figures is to our right. We're flying in this formation because it makes us look like an authority fight cruiser on sensors. That will dissuade any pirates from coming our way if they manage to glimpse us. Just adjust our course and speed if Blade does. Can you do that?"

Marisol nodded. "What are you going to say to them?"

"They need to know what to expect to keep them from panicking. That's the last thing we need right now."

"I should do that."

"No. I need to get to know them and make certain they know the rules. Big won't tolerate them upsetting his female or anyone else living on base. Blade's female is human, and Rod just picked up her parents, so they are living at our base, too."

The shock on her face was cute. Her brown eyes widened, and her mouth parted.

"I don't have many details since we always speak in code and keep our communications short, but I'm kept updated on what's happening there. I won't be gone long. I'm transferring control to your console now."

He did that and stood, releasing the lock on the cockpit door. It opened to reveal the black-haired clone with grayish-colored eyes. Free encroached into his personal space, forcing him back. The male retreated a few steps. Free stopped, closing the doors behind him.

"Who are you?"

"I'm MC-1."

Free stepped to the side, taking in the other three clones. They stood farther back in the living space. All of them had black hair, but the women had different colored eyes, while the males could have been related with their unique gray eyes. That didn't surprise him since clone models tended to have similar coloring and looks, seemingly selected for whatever duties they'd been created for. It helped knowledgeable humans guess what they were at a glance.

"Who are they? Introduce me," Free demanded.

MC-1 put a little more space between them, pointing out his fellow clones. "MC-2 is the other male. The shortest female is MC-3, and then there's MC-4."

"My name is Free. I was an F Clone created to work in the finance department of Clone World. The staff named me Freak. I hated being called that, but as you know, humans didn't care if we were content with the names they assigned to us." He paused. "I'm guessing you're all called M's because Marisol said you were her medical team. What does the C stand for?"

"Medical classified, and we were numbered in the order of being activated from shipment," MC-2 informed him. "We were solely assigned to care for Ms. Florigo. She is the reason we exist."

"You have three days until we join other clones. I'd think about changing what you're called into something you like by then. I'd resent having a number as part of my name, but that's up to you." Free took a deep breath. "Never forget that Marisol is the reason you are alive. That won't change just because you aren't on Clone World anymore. I won't tolerate anyone hurting her. Never forget that."

MC-1 inched closer to the other three.

Free didn't blame him. He was threatening them. "I'm not trying to be a dick, but I like to be transparent and concise with my words. I'm taking the four of you to my home. There are other clones there, as well as a few humans. They are not like the ones we interacted with on Clone World. One of those humans is in a romantic relationship with a B Clone. Blade taught me how to fight." He paused for effect. "You do not want to insult or harm his human. He'd make you regret it."

MC-3 braved speaking. "We won't cause any trouble. Our goal is to fit in. Where are we going? Is it a planet?"

Free studied her, judging that she was being honest. "We're going to a mining station built at the core of a moon crater. It housed thousands of human workers when it was still operational. There are only a handful of us living there right now."

None of the four said a word, just staring at him.

"Some living quarters were designed for solo humans, but there were also families with children who once lived there. I've seen units with as many as five bedrooms. You'll be given a choice of what you prefer. Marisol said you lived in an isolated cottage on Clone World. I'll assume it was small and cramped. I shared a bunk room with the five clones I escaped with. It was unsettling when we first slept apart. That's why you have options. No one will tell you when you have to sleep, with whom, what to wear, or when to eat. Freedom is about having choices."

"I would like to sleep with MC-4," MC-2 informed him. "Would we be allowed to share the same bed?" He held out his hand to the female.

She instantly went to his side and clasped his hand, appearing almost frightened. "Are we in trouble for asking that?"

"No." Free wanted to put them at ease. "I'm in love with Marisol. I plan to share a bed and home with her. You can do whatever you like as long as it's consensual. We have common rules at our home base. We respect and treat each other well. Big is ultimately in charge. He's a B Clone. Think of him as our leader. He's fair, kind, and will do what's best for all of us."

MC-1 didn't seem to like that. He walked over to the shortest female and glared at Free. "What kind of orders will he give us? What will he expect of us? I thought we would be without masters once we escaped."

Free knew his eyebrows shot up. "When I say he's our leader, I mean he's the one who will help you settle in and find tasks you like to do. We all pitch in to keep the station running while living there."

That seemed to make the male calm. "Understood."

"It's going to take three days for us to arrive where we're going. Food is in the kitchen, and you're welcome to eat as much as you like. There are two bedrooms. The one with the large bed is mine. I plan to have Marisol use it. There is a second bedroom with two bunks for your use. Space is limited on my shuttle. I apologize for that. Maybe you can sleep in shifts until we arrive at the station or share the bunks since you are a set of couples. The bunks should fit two if you sleep closely together. Do you have any other questions? I'd like to get back to Marisol. We have a lot of things to discuss."

"Do you have any spare clothing?"

He nodded at MC-2. "I'll get some for you now. I don't have anything that would fit the females, but you're welcome to alter the clothing. Feel free to shower. The water tanks are full enough for us to reach home without running out."

Free showed them to the second bedroom and grabbed some of his clothing from his room for them to share. He hurried, wanting to get back to Marisol. It was highly doubtful that the pirates would find them after all the course changes they'd made, but he wouldn't relax until they were home.

He entered the cockpit to find Marisol staring at him with a worried expression. "Your clones are fine. I gave them some of my clothing, showed them where to sleep, and they know what to expect once we reach home base." He retook his seat, transferring flight control back to his console.

"You looked a little mad when you left."

He didn't deny it. "They needed to know who is in charge. I didn't like how pushy MC-1 acted. I understand his protectiveness for the other clones since he's probably led them since they were activated, but they aren't on Clone World anymore. He needed to be told that Big is ultimately in charge now."

"What's he's like? Figures was the only one I knew in the group you left with."

"Big's code name is Father. It's the role he took with our team after we escaped. He looks out for all of us and plays the peacekeeper when any of us have conflicts. He's also the one who stayed behind at the mining station when the rest of us went seeking adventure. Big made certain we always had a home to return to."

"What have you been doing for the past three years?"

"Existing," he admitted. "I wasn't emotionally stable when I believed I'd lost you forever. The others didn't understand the loss of love. It drove me into wanting to be away from them."

Sympathy shone in her eyes. "That must have been difficult for you."

"I wasn't easy to live with, and I knew it. It's why I felt I needed to leave. I stayed away because I didn't want the depression and bitterness I felt to make life for the others more difficult."

"Do you want to live with them again? You don't have to make that choice just because of me. I'm happy we're together. It doesn't matter to me where we live."

"I want us to live with the others. It's too dangerous for us to continue to live on my shuttle and travel around. I refuse to risk your life. The mining station affords us safety in numbers, and we're able to protect it if anyone ever remembers that it is there."

"I look forward to meeting everyone, and it will be nice to possibly make friends."

Marisol had once told Free that she didn't have any of those when he'd asked if she would miss anyone from Clone World after they left. She'd explained that humans believed she could gain them better jobs and more pay. They only pretended to like her because she was a Florigo.

"I'm certain you will make friends with the other females, Marisol. Everything will be better."

She smiled. "We'll finally get the future together we always dreamed about."

Emotion choked him up, and he had to look away. "Yes."

Motion had him turn back to Marisol. She rose from the other chair and came to him. It surprised Free when she sat on his lap and twisted to put their faces inches apart. Her hands lightly clutched his shoulders. He liked having her so close.

"Is the cockpit door locked?"

"Yes." Free had done that when he'd entered, not expecting any interruptions after he'd had his talk with the M Clones, but he didn't know them well enough to be certain.

Her smile widened. "No one is going to interrupt us. I'm going to kiss you."

"Wait!" He wanted that badly, but he needed to do one thing first. He reached around Marisol's body and sent a low signal hail to Blade. The male answered immediately.

"Is something wrong?"

"Can I link auto-control to you?"

The male chuckled. "Of course. Nothing has shown up on long-range sensors. I don't foresee any problems. Just listen for communications in case that changes."

"Thank you." Free had the shuttle's computer establish a link with Blade's Varlius model. It took over piloting his shuttle.

"I've got you," Blade informed him.

"I'm out." Free cut communications, knowing they were in good hands and Blade would let them know if any danger arose. He reached up and cupped Marisol's face gently. "Now I am all yours."

She leaned in close and closed her eyes. He remembered that she said humans did that during kissing. Free's heart raced from excitement as her soft lips lightly brushed against his. His entire body went haywire when she deepened the kiss, her tongue tasting his.

His body began to respond, too. He felt his dick stiffen and sweat break out over his skin. She made him feel hot in the best way. Marisol's fingers dove into his short hair, tugging a little on it while she massaged his scalp. It all felt amazing. She even pressed against him tighter until he could feel the mounds of her breasts pushing against his chest. She was the one who finally broke away.

"Did you have sex with someone?"

"No."

Marisol smiled. "Good. I've always wanted to be your first." She slid off his lap and started removing her clothing.

It stunned him. "We should go to my cabin."

"You need to keep an ear out for Blade in case you have to fly this shuttle again. We don't need a bed. Trust me. I've thought for a long time about all the things I want to do with you. Get naked with me."

Free didn't need to be told twice. He bent forward, yanking off his boots. He wore a spacesuit that opened in the front. That was what he wore any time he expected trouble in case there was a battle. It still amazed him that Marisol had been waiting and seeking him.

He almost ripped the protective suit off in his haste to be rid of anything that impeded him and Marisol from touching skin-to-skin. It was a dream come true for him. He couldn't stop staring as she revealed her beautiful body. Marisol appeared soft all over, and he itched to touch every inch of her.

A question rose, but he refused to speak it. Free didn't want to know if she'd met someone else while they'd been apart. It would break his heart. He removed the suit all the way and stood bare in front of her, hoping she liked the sight of him.

Her gaze roamed from his feet up to his stiff dick. "You're the sexiest man I've ever seen," she murmured. She studied his upper body. "You're also super muscular for an accountant, Free."

"I do a lot more than sit at a desk now."

"Let's pretend we're back in the office. Take a seat."

Free normally wouldn't place his bare ass on the pilot seat, but he instantly sat. He'd do anything Marisol wanted. She stepped closer. He was very distracted with her pink nipples right there in front of him. She took his breath away.

"I want to touch you."

"I'm yours," he responded, finding that it was difficult to speak. Her beauty tongue-tied him.

Marisol placed her hands on his chest, lightly exploring him. Free reached down, blindly found the button to convert the pilot seat into a bed, and slid off it. He wrapped an arm around her waist, amused at her surprised expression, right as he lifted her off her feet. He moved them both out of the way as the chair flattened next to them.

"Free?"

"I did research. I memorized everything I wanted to try on you if ever given the chance. Do I have your permission?"

Marisol clung to him. "Yes."

That caused him to smile. "Good."

He laid her out on the padded flat chair and pressed his lips against hers. Marisol moaned against his tongue after he deepened the kiss. He let his hands roam her body where he could reach. Her skin was as soft as it looked.

Free broke the kiss to go for her throat next, trailing his lips and tongue down to her shoulder before going lower. He paid extensive attention to her nipples, loving the way they stiffened, and more moans came from Marisol. He knew he was doing everything right from all the indications with the way she shifted and writhed on the chair.

Free kissed her belly. His gaze roamed her beautiful body, and his fingertips brushed over her hips. He froze, though, when he realized what was missing, leaning in to study each side of her hips.

"Marisol, I don't think you are a clone. It doesn't matter to me, but later, I'll be questioning your M Clones."

"I'm sure DJD was paid extra to remove the normal scar that shows where I was grown inside a vat and to avoid stamping me with the product tattoo so I couldn't easily be identified as a clone."

"You're sure?"

Marisol held his gaze. "I was conscious and watched MC-3 give me a plasma transfusion. I'm a clone since I didn't die."

That convinced him. It really didn't matter though. He loved Marisol regardless of what she physically was. Free leaned in, letting his hands roam her body once more. He loved the taste of her skin, the way she shifted on the converted bed and the soft moans she made.

He focused on her sex when Marisol parted her legs as if she couldn't stay still. Free used his thumb to explore the seam of her pussy, discovering that she was wet and almost ready to take his dick. He explored the fleshy bud above her slip, growing more excited when her moans became louder. It seemed his research had been correct. A female became highly aroused when her clit was stimulated.

Her scent of need grew stronger, and he leaned in, pushed her legs farther apart, and removed his thumb. He replaced it with his tongue. He loved the taste of her and the way her fingers dove into his blond hair, encouraging him to continue. They both seemed to love oral sex. Her getting it and him giving.

"Free, I'm going to…"

He grew more aggressive with his tongue, licking and sucking on the swollen bud. Marisol's hips bucked, and it seemed as if she were trying to get away from his mouth. He used his hands to pin her in place, not stopping until she loudly cried out his name and her body spasmed under him. He pulled back, grinning from the knowledge that he'd just made her climax.

"You liked that."

"I loved that." Marisol tugged on his hair, which she still gripped, trying to pull him up her body.

He climbed onto the converted bed, getting between her thighs. Marisol welcomed him, releasing his hair to clutch at his shoulders instead. She also spread her legs, bringing them up and wrapping them around his waist. His very hard dick nudged against her sex, and he adjusted his hips, reached down between them to help position his shaft, but then froze. He held her gaze.

"Do you want me?"

"Yes. Claim me as yours, Free."

That was all he needed as he slowly sank inside her body. A deep groan burst from him at the feel of her heated sex taking him. She was hot, wet, and tight. Clones were told they were soulless beings with no deity, but he suddenly believed in heaven. It was Marisol and the pleasure he felt at being inside her as she wrapped her limbs tighter around him.

They fit perfectly. He braced both hands on the bed to get traction and started to move. It felt incredible, and Marisol seemed to agree as her fingernails dug into her skin. Her moaning of his name urged him to move faster, fucking her deeper. Free let instinct take over until he felt her vaginal muscles clenching and milking his shaft. He cried out her name as he came, emptying his seed inside her body.

"Yes!" Marisol found her release, too.

He had to resist collapsing on top of her as they struggled to recover from the best experience of his life. Every bone and muscle in his body seemed to feel liquified in the aftermath of such extreme physical pleasure. Marisol made him feel strong and ultimately weak at the same time. He wouldn't change a thing.

Free opened his eyes to find Marisol smiling at him.

She licked her lips. "I love you."

"I love you too, Marisol. I also love sex."

That had her laughing. It felt strange but good to have her body shaking that way while they were so intimately still connected. It triggered him to want to do it all over again. Desire heated his blood, and he adjusted his arm to free his hand, cupping her face. He took her mouth in a deep kiss.

Marisol wrapped her limbs tight around him again and started to roll her hips, suggestively rubbing them together. Free began to fuck her again. They had a lot of time to make up for, and he planned to learn everything that pleased his female. He'd read about a lot of different sexual positions. They'd have to try them out to learn her favorites.

Chapter Nine

Marisol woke, sprawled on top of Free. A faint beeping had pulled her from a deep sleep. He must have heard it, too, since his eyes opened, and a low groan came from his parted lips.

She sat up, straddling his body. She'd learned every inch of it over the past few days. They'd made love as if their lives depended on it. Her muscles were achy even after sleeping, but she had zero complaints.

The buzzing noise came again, distracting her from admiring his muscular, sexy body. Her gaze ran over the nearest console. "We're being hailed."

Free sat up, touching the control on the side of the converted bed, and it began to shift into a pilot seat once more. "It's Blade." He leaned forward, put one arm around her to keep her on his lap, and opened a channel.

"Yes?"

"It's time for you to take back control of your shuttle. I can't pilot us both through the entrance."

Marisol brushed a kiss on his cheek after hearing what Blade had to say. Free needed to fly so they could dock with the mining station. She wiggled her hips, forcing him to let her go. She stood, reaching for her discarded clothing resting in the other seat.

They'd spent the last three days making love, learning about each other's bodies, and enjoying being together. The only time they left the cockpit was to eat, shower, or use the bathroom. She'd barely spoken to the M Clones.

Free quickly dressed. "Why the scowl? You are going to like our new home and the people there. I promise you'll make friends."

"I'm feeling guilty about how little time I've spent with the M's. We've been acting like irresponsible teenagers lost to their raging hormones."

Free chuckled. "That is an accurate description of how I've felt. You are intoxicating, my love." His humor faded. "They are fully grown clones who aren't newly activated. You're not their leader or their parent."

"I still feel responsible for them."

"I understand. Let them know we'll be docking in..." he studied the console. "Ten minutes."

"I'm going to use the bathroom before I return." Marisol went to leave.

Free grabbed her hand. "Hurry back. I want you at my side."

"Is there any danger where we're going?" She suddenly felt worried. It was possible that the other clones wouldn't be accepting of having a Florigo in their midst. Her grandfather had caused clones a lot of misery.

"I just want you next to me. There's nothing to worry about."

She relaxed again. "Okay. I'll be right back." Marisol released his hand, unlocked the cockpit door, and opened it. None of the M's were in the living space. She used the bathroom first and then went to their cabin door, touching a button to let them know she was there.

In seconds, MC-1 opened it. It was apparent that he'd been sleeping. He only wore sleeping shorts. Marisol kept her gaze on his face. "We're about to dock with the mining station. You all should get dressed and ready to embark."

MC-3 came up to his side. She wore an oversized T-shirt, also looking as if she'd just awoken. "MC-4 and I only have our security guard outfits to wear. None of your male's clothing fit us."

"Wear your security guard outfits," Marisol decided. "I'm sorry we didn't really have time to grab all our stuff from the other shuttle. I don't have any spare clothing to give you since that bag was left in the sleeping cabin."

"Won't the other clones be alarmed seeing our females wearing human outfits from Clone World?" MC-1 scowled. "The other clones might attack them, believing they are humans coming to capture them."

"I doubt that will happen. I'm sure it's fine if your females just wear Free's T-shirts. They fall long enough to cover them down to their thighs. Free has assured me we'll all have access to clothing soon." Marisol wanted to get back to the cockpit.

"I don't want any of the males believing they can seduce our females into a relationship." MC-1 looked mad at the very concept.

"All the males there already have females," Marisol informed him. "Free has been telling me about his friends. "That's not something you need to be concerned with."

"Humans always take what they want from us. Your clone mentioned that a few humans will be there. I don't want them trying to take MC-3 from me."

Marisol's patience wore thin. She really wanted to get back to Free. "Only one human will be a man, and he's married. They are the parents of the woman who is with Blade. Stop worrying so much, and get ready to dock. Everything will be fine."

MC-1 still didn't look convinced.

"I got us off Clone World and found the escaped clones, didn't I? You need to listen to me now, too," Marisol snapped. "Get dressed in whatever you want. We'll be there soon. Also, try to be a little less paranoid and more friendly. We're going to live with everyone we're about to meet. Remember that. First bad impressions tend to stick with people. So do good ones."

She spun away, hurrying back to the cockpit. The doors remained wide open. She entered, staring out the front screen as they flew directly behind the larger shuttle in front of them. Free glanced back at her.

"Is everything alright?"

"Yes." She took a seat, belting in. "They were sleeping. I had to wake them up."

"I'm glad we're not the only ones who have spent so much time in bed."

Marisol smiled. "I doubt they were doing all the things we have since both couples were sharing a room. You should have let me give them your bedroom. It's not like we used it."

"I wanted you to have the option to be comfortable."

"I was very content to sleep on top of you. That big mattress in your cabin wasn't tempting since you weren't sharing it with me."

Free smiled, his attention focused on sensors. "We'll have use of a real bed very soon. I would bet that Big never reassigned the living quarters I chose in the past. I think you'll like it."

"I'm sure I will."

It was pitch dark out the front view screen. Her gaze dropped to the console in front of her. It showed that they were traveling through a wide tunnel passage of what appeared to be surrounded by solid rock. Masses of boulders blocked some of it, and they had to fly around them.

"We'll be there soon," Free assured her.

Marisol nodded, seeing that Blade's largest ship was ahead of them and the other one behind them. It made her a little nervous that they seemed to be flying so close together, but she trusted Free's piloting skills. Soon enough, she saw that the tunnel ended. They'd reached the clone's home base.

All three shuttles docked, and Free shut down his engines. Marisol reached for her belt to unbuckle.

"Wait." Free turned off their gravity stabilizers.

Marisol felt her body tug downward for a split second, but then that strange feeling disappeared just as quickly.

"Natural and artificial gravity isn't completely in sync with my shuttle. It's safe now." Free stood, holding out his hand to her.

Marisol clutched onto Free as they left the cockpit. The M Clones were assembled in the living space. The two females wore Clone World security uniforms for the human staff, and both males sported Free's spare clothing.

"Have you decided on names?" Free addressed them all.

"We're keeping what we're used to for now," MC-1 informed him. "We may change our minds later."

"There is some comfort in familiarity." Free inclined his head. "Let's go. I'm certain that Big is eager to greet us."

"Remember what I said," Marisol told the M Clones. "These are our people. Even the human ones. Be on your best behavior, and don't allow paranoia to take hold. We're safe here."

MC-1 frowned.

"I trust Free with my life and yours." Marisol showed the four clones her hand linked with Free's. "It's going to be fine."

"We'll follow your lead," MC-1 finally sighed.

"Good enough." Marisol smiled up at Free. "I'm ready. Are you?"

"Yes." Free led them to the docking door in his cargo hold and punched in a code. The exit door unsealed, and they had to step a few feet forward. That secondary door automatically slid open, revealing a huge interior docking port.

A couple exited the shuttle docked behind theirs. The male was tall with blond hair and blue eyes. Marisol instantly recognized him. It was Figures. The shorter woman at his side had white hair and bright green eyes.

Marisol looked left to see a B Clone exit from the largest shuttle. It was easy to identify what he was with his above-average height, overly muscular body, and black hair. Those models were built to intimidate for security purposes. It had to be Blade.

Motion drew her attention as a group of people entered the docking port area. It was another B Clone with a blonde woman. A second woman with long, wild brown hair broke from the others, running at Blade. He opened his arms as she nearly slammed into him. The B Clone easily lifted her off her feet, kissing her eagerly for all to see. No one needed to tell Marisol that they were a couple. One who had been apart and were happy to see each other again.

Her gaze went to the older couple hanging back. The woman looked enough like the long-haired brunette that she guessed they had to be the parents. It helped Marisol figure out who the humans were.

The B Clone with the blonde approached, them holding hands. His attention was focused on Free, a smile on his lips. Marisol knew that had to be Big.

"It is so good to see you again, Free. I've missed your scowling face." Big stopped feet away. "Do you hug?"

Free shook his head. "I only like Marisol touching me."

That's when Big's dark blue eyes fixed on her. Marisol met his gaze. "Hello. You must be Big. We never formally met on Clone World."

"I'm Gemma." The blonde at his side smiled at her. "Welcome to your new home, Miss Florigo. And thank you so much for helping these guys get away from Clone World. I've heard about what you did. None of us would be here if it weren't for you."

"Call me Marisol. I'm no longer a Florigo, thankfully. I'd like to introduce you to the four clones that escaped with me. They are all nervous, as you can imagine. I promised them they'd have better lives. Please don't make me a liar."

Big's eyes widened, seeming surprised by her words.

"They are going to love it here," Gemma quickly gushed. "I am so happy to see more people. Our community is really small, so every new person is extremely welcome. I don't know if Free told you about the mining station, but a few thousand people used to live here. Now we're…" she glanced around. "Fourteen."

Marisol introduced the M's, learning Hailey and Anna's names. Both women remained quiet. The older human couple stayed back. Her gaze kept going to them.

"Those are my parents," Hailey whispered. "Sam and Klista. They were worried it might upset some of you because we're the only humans here. We come from Maglis. It's a mining planet, and I never once visited Clone World."

Blade hugged her closer to his side. "Sam and Klista have no bias against our kind or hold prejudices. That's what Hailey is attempting to get across." He seemed to be studying the M's.

"They were my medics," Marisol admitted. "My highly classified medic team."

That drew everyone's attention. Big was the one to speak. "Are you ill? Is that why you decided to finally join us and be with Free? The mining company took their surgical unit with them after abandoning the station but left behind some medical equipment. We'll do our best to help you."

Free tensed at her side. Marisol clung to his hand to keep him from moving. He looked upset. "I didn't join up with you before because I died shortly after reaching Barlish station. I couldn't get into an escape pod to reach Free because my body was being secretly flown to DJD Clone Corp to have an unblanked copy of me made. I'm not sick. I'm a clone."

The shock on Big's face was almost comical. His expression matched that of Figures and Blade, too. The others, besides her M Clones, just seemed stunned.

"I didn't know the truth until recently." Marisol shared how she'd discovered the truth and why she'd brought her medic team with her. She gazed at the white-haired woman. "Learning that Figures had used that secret fund to order an unblanked copy of you is what alerted me that at least one of them had survived and how to find him. I guess I should thank you."

Anna smiled. "I wouldn't say I'm a copy. I used to be old. Now I'm all new and shiny. My Fig has a generous heart, and I'm glad his good deed of giving me a second chance at life brought you all here."

Figures put his arm around her and drew her closer to his side. "I was desperate to save Anna in any way possible. She was kind to me, and I wanted to spend more time with her. Then she captured my heart."

Marisol couldn't help but smile. It was clear that the two were in love. The older human couple finally approached.

"We prepared a feast," the woman announced. "I'm Klista. Sam and I have taken on the parental role for everyone here. I hope you don't find that presumptuous. We just want to make you feel welcome and at home."

Marisol smiled. "Thank you. We appreciate that."

"Clones don't have parents," MC-1 commented.

Marisol shot him a dirty look. "It seems like we do now. That's wonderful. A feast means lots of food. I'm really looking forward to that after exiting off nutrient bars for so long."

"We do appreciate that." Free backed her up. "I am hungry."

Marisol did a head count. There were fourteen people. "Where are the R clones?"

Big answered. "Rod was here but left to go investigate what DJD Clone Corp is doing by opening what we believe is a secret laboratory on a space station. Ram is currently out of communication with us, but Rod told us not to be alarmed."

That intrigued Marisol. "What kind of secret laboratory and why on a space station?"

"That is what Rod plans to find out. Earth banned creating and testing unblanked clones. We're afraid they are going to attempt something equally as horrific on our kind," Blade shared.

"I hope my grandfather has nothing to do with this." Marisol felt sick at the thought.

"Why would you say that?" Free turned toward her, his gaze holding hers.

"He's the one who is their number one customer. He's also ordered a lot of illegal clones. Look at me. I survived thinking I was still human for over three years. DJD Clone Corp obviously is aware of that since they grew this body and transferred my birth chip." She held up her other hand he wasn't holding. "I passed every security scanner I went through."

Big suddenly moved closer. "What are you talking about?"

Marisol turned to him and held out her palm. "I still have my original birth chip. DJD Clone Corp was somehow able to do the impossible by transferring it."

"What in the hell is that?" Anna had moved closer, too.

"Humans who leave or live away from Earth are embedded with a data chip inside the palms of their hands shortly after birth," Big explained. "They are supposed to be coded to that human's DNA. Removing it, transferring it into another body, or even attempting to hack the data on one is supposed to destroy it. The human authorities use scanners to safeguard that clones aren't permitted to enter Earth, some other planets, and most space stations near Earth."

"I don't think I had one of those when I was still human," Anna admitted.

"They began using them about fifty years ago," Marisol told her. "You should have been given one at birth."

"Oh. That explains it. I was born way before then." Anna smiled at the M Clones. "You four are being so quiet. I haven't been here too long. I'd be happy to give you a tour of the station after we eat."

"We both will," Figures offered. "I'm sure you'll need clothing and other things to make you feel at home."

"Speaking of, during dinner, you can tell me what sleeping arrangements you prefer." Big met their gazes, staring at Free the longest. "Your quarters haven't been touched except I had your bots clean and Magna stock your kitchen."

That perked Marisol's interest. "Who is Magna?"

Gemma was the one to answer. "Not who. What. Magna is a silver robot that cooks. Some of the nicer apartments have them. It freaked me out the first time I saw it because I watched way too many horror movies."

"Let's move this to our quarters and eat while the food is hot. I didn't use a Magna to cook. I actually enjoy doing that myself. We'll all exchange stories and get to know each other better." Klista motioned everyone to follow her and her human husband. "Come on."

Free lifted Marisol's hand, kissing the back of it. "We'll eat and then go to our quarters. I think you'll like where we'll live."

"I know I will." The mining station would be her new home, and the people living there hopefully would become her friends.

Chapter Ten

The dinner had been great. Even better, Marisol really liked the clones and humans she spent time with while they ate. Some of the couples had shared their stories. It amazed her that her grandfather had ordered an illegally unblanked singer from Earth, but DJD Clone Corp had messed up. They'd stolen the wrong body of a woman with the same name. Big had found Gemma as she was being shipped to Clone World.

Free led them to one of the cabins, pressed his palm print to it, and the double doors opened. Marisol gawked a bit as they entered the upscale living room. It was nicely furnished and had an open floor plan, so the kitchen was within sight.

"This used to belong to one of the humans with an important job. There are two bedrooms, two and a half baths, and an office," he summarized. "There is a Magna in the kitchen to do our cooking."

That made Marisol smile. Gemma, her new friend, had warned her. "I've met those types of androids before. We don't have them on Clone World, but other resort planets and some of the nicer space stations I've stayed at do. I'm glad we have one. I'm a terrible cook."

"I am as well."

"I kind of guessed that since all you had on your shuttle was nutrient bars and those freeze-dried packs you add heated water to."

He took her hand, leading her through the living space and down a hallway. The main bedroom was also roomy, nicely furnished, and had a resort-like spa bath. She had her choice of a steam shower, real water, and even a bathtub big enough to fit two. "I'm surprised you chose this for yourself."

"Big insisted. There are a total of ten luxury suites, and only six of us. I always believed it was too much space for an individual, but he convinced us to claim them as ours."

"How did he do that?" She released his hand and took a seat on the oversized bed. The mattress was like sinking into a cloud.

"He reminded us that we wanted a better future and that expansive living quarters were achieving that goal."

She smiled. "I like it."

"That's all that matters." He locked gazes with her. "The M's seemed to relax and settle in better."

"I was worried about them, but dinner was a great way to break the ice and get to know each other better. I really like Sam and Klista."

"They seem to be good humans."

"Anna might be my favorite. She's so happy to be alive."

Free took a seat next to her. "I'm very glad that Figures decided to rescue her in the only way he knew how after she died in his arms."

"It triggered me realizing you were still alive, at least one of you, and refusing to eat my drugged dinner."

"Yes. How are you adjusting to being a clone?"

Marisol kicked off her shoes, getting more comfortable. They were in for the evening. There was a planned tour of the station in the morning. Gemma and Hailey were going to help her, the M's, and Anna get new wardrobes. She was looking forward to that. The bag she'd packed with clothes had been left behind, and that had left her stuck wearing Free's oversized shirts and the outfit she'd worn when he'd come for her.

"I think it makes it easier that I've been living as a clone for almost three years without knowing it. The bottom line, I'm still me. I honestly had no clue I wasn't human anymore."

"What about your menstrual cycles? I'm aware that humans have those. Clones don't."

Marisol froze, her mind stunned with realization. "I take birth control shots that prevent me from having periods, but..."

Free must have sensed something was wrong because he slid off the bed, kneeling before her. "What's wrong? You have gone unusually pale. But what?"

It was too shocking for her to even comprehend.

"Marisol?"

"You have a health center on this station, right?"

"Yes."

"We need to go there now."

"Why? What's wrong? Talk to me."

"I missed the shot I get every three months last year when I was working on a big project. I started my period." She stared into his eyes. "Clones are sterile. You're right. They don't have periods. But I did. I had one."

"You said you were given clone plasma."

"I was." She felt nauseous as the suspicion she had seemed more viable. "DJD Clone Corp breaks the rules for my gramps all the time. What if they created me without safeguards and my reproductive organs work?"

He leaned in close, placing his hands on her legs to give comfort. "You believe your grandfather asked them to do this? Make it so you could have children?"

"I told you that he asked me to have a baby when I turned twenty-five. I refused and told him I'd think about it when I turned thirty. That's coming up in a few months. He loved having me under his thumb. The thought of having more family members he could control and manipulate would appeal to him. Gramps would have hated to lose that option when I died."

"Rico Florigo didn't have to. I agree that DJD Clone Corp would do anything he asked. He can certainly afford to bribe them well." Free caressed her legs. "Does it matter what he did? You're you, Marisol. I am sterile. We won't be able to have children even if they gave you the ability. Not unless you wish to leave me to find a human."

Marisol reached out and cupped his face. "You're who I want. It just shocked me. You're right. It doesn't change anything. I'll just have to deal with periods after my last shot wears off. We already have at least one menstruating human living here. I'm sure Hailey and possibly her mom have programmed one of the shops to print out supplies to handle their periods."

"Do you want to go to the health clinic?"

She calmed, the surprise fading. "No. The more I think about it, I'm certain that's exactly what he did. Gramps never liked being denied anything. I don't need medical confirmation."

"We could find a donor to—"

"No. I have never wanted children after everything I experienced. You're all I want."

Free leaned in. "I love you." He kissed her.

Marisol happily pushed away all thoughts and kissed him back. All their dreams were coming true. They were free to love and to be together. She leaned back, pulling Free onto the bed with her.

He rolled them until he was under her. Both frantically tugged at each other's clothing, wanting to get naked. It was sweet that he was always so careful with her and worried he might crush or harm her in some way. She had to break the kiss to tear her shirt off over her head.

"I love you too." Her gaze wandered over his sexy body as he pulled off his shirt, revealing his muscled chest and arms. "Our life is going to be perfect."

"It will," he agreed.

Up next… R Clones

About the Author

NY Times and USA Today Bestselling Author

I'm a full-time author. I've been lucky enough to have spent over three decades with the love of my life. I'm addicted to iced coffee, the occasional candy bar (or two), and trying to get at least five hours of sleep at night.

I love to write all kinds of stories. The best part about writing is that real life is always uncertain, always tossing things at us that we have no control over, but when writing you can make sure there's always a happy ending.

For the most up to date information, please visit my website. www.LaurannDohner.com

Made in United States
North Haven, CT
12 August 2024